img_1

"WHY WAS IT SO IMPORTANT TO GET BLACKWELL INTO THE HUNT?"

Before he spoke the Huntmaster looked closely at Simmons, the man who had recruited Blackwell. "His importance is positional. His characteristics further a deeper plan. Blackwell's actions will predispose rather than set up certain moves from the other side. The times have conspired to produce a need for him. America is in a period of rapid change. Laws decriminalizing all aspects of the drug business are now on the books. Suicide is no longer against the law. Murder has been officially condoned under an increasing number of circumstances. Legislation for legalization of the Hunt will be brought forward by our friends in Congress within the year. At this stage of our development we must take certain risks."

"Still," Simmons said, "it's a bit hard on Blackwell, isn't it?"

The Huntmaster's look was at once gentle and unyielding. "He might come out of it alive. Stranger things have happened. . . ."

"The key words with Sheckley are clever, deadly cool. . . . I don't know anyone else in SF who has written quite so many really classic stories."
—Spider Robinson

"Real blood flows in his vein of surrealism."
—*The Times Literary Supplement*

HUNTER/
VICTIM

· · · · · · · · ·

Robert Sheckley

A SIGNET BOOK

NEW AMERICAN LIBRARY

NAL BOOKS ARE AVAILABLE AT QUANTITY DISCOUNTS WHEN
USED TO PROMOTE PRODUCTS OR SERVICES. FOR INFORMA-
TION PLEASE WRITE TO PREMIUM MARKETING DIVISION, NEW
AMERICAN LIBRARY, 1633 BROADWAY, NEW YORK, NEW YORK
10019.

SIGNET TRADEMARK REG. U.S. PAT. OFF. AND FOREIGN COUNTRIES
REGISTERED TRADEMARK—MARCA REGISTRADA
HECHO EN CHICAGO, U.S.A.

SIGNET, SIGNET CLASSIC, MENTOR, ONYX, PLUME, MERIDIAN
and NAL BOOKS are published by NAL PENGUIN INC.,
1633 Broadway, New York, New York 10019

First Printing, January, 1988

1 2 3 4 5 6 7 8 9

PRINTED IN THE UNITED STATES OF AMERICA

To my children

ACKNOWLEDGMENTS:

I would like to thank these people for their assistance:

Norman Schwarz of the Hotel Norman, Miami Beach, Florida
Agustin "Augie" Enriquez of Combat Corner in Portland, Oregon
Sergeant Ed Kirsch of Beaverton, Oregon

With special thanks to N. Lee Wood

PART ONE

THE MAKING
OF A HUNTER

1 • • • • •

Frank Blackwell and his wife, Claire, spent most of the last day of their Paris trip in the hotel room having one of those interminable arguments in which neither side remembers exactly what the subject of discussion is any longer, but each knows that the other is deeply wrong and should be made to understand that.

The argument had reached the stage of long silences, with Blackwell shaking his head frequently, as though commenting to an invisible audience on the strange intractability of women, and Claire, for her part, stared into the middle distance in the manner of heroines from all times and ages.

Outside the curtained windows, Paris stewed in its miasma of self-congratulation and diesel fumes.

"And what about yesterday, in the Metro?" Claire said, suddenly remembering why she was angry at Frank.

"The Metro? What about the Metro?" Blackwell said.

"The girl you gave your seat to. That tart with the black stockings and those big boobs you couldn't keep your eyes off of. *That* girl."

"Oh, that one," Blackwell said. "But what was wrong with my giving her my seat?"

"The Metro wasn't even crowded!" Claire cried. "She could have sat anywhere in the goddam car!"

"She just didn't seem to realize that," Blackwell said. "She struck me as very naive."

"Naive! Oh, you bastard!" Claire said.

She stared at him with loathing.

He stared back with incomprehension.

And the funny thing was, neither of them liked to fight. Both felt that one of the worst things about their relationship was the way the other always insisted on quarreling.

Like many couples, they had a regular anthology of unpleasant topics, and one invariably led to another.

Nonetheless, they were very much in love.

Blackwell was a man of medium height with moments of tallness. Straight, mouse-brown hair. Receding hairline. Steel-rimmed glasses through which glinted the mild hazel eyes of the intelligent myopic.

Claire was a good-looking chunky blonde of the Greenwich Village waitress variety with a taste for Turner's watercolors and foreign films, as long as they weren't dubbed. She was a loving woman with a lot of class, which she showed now by saying, contrary to expectation, "Oh, Frank, this really is silly, isn't it? What do you say we put this argument on hold and go down and get some lunch?"

Their Paris trip had not been entirely a success.

First of all, it had rained steadily for the first three days.

Second, Claire had gotten an upset stomach from the rich and unfamiliar cuisine. That took care of days four and five.

Then Frank's traveler's checks were stolen from his jacket pocket, probably while negotiating the crowds between Montparnasse and St.-Germain. Luckily he had recorded their numbers. But he still had to waste the better part of a day getting a refund. Now Claire carried the money and their passports in the leather shoulder bag that she never released her grip on.

Their hotel, Le Cygne, was a quaint little place just a few streets from Notre Dame. It was charming in that rundown ratty way the French have perfected. You entered a small lobby lit by fifteen-watt light bulbs. The concierge, a bulky woman dressed in black bombazine, had her own quarters just off the lobby. Her door was always open, so that she could watch everybody coming and going and gossip about them to the neighbors or the police. After identifying you, she gave you your key, which was attached to a large rubber ball by a brass fixture to prevent you from slipping it into your pocket and walking off with it. Key in hand, you turned left and went up a curving staircase, pitched at a perilous angle, to your room, probably on the fifth floor. Once inside, by walking across the quaintly tilted floor and opening the tall white-curtained french windows, you could look out over the rooftops of Paris. And that moment, unduplicated anywhere else in the world, made it all worthwhile.

Frank and Claire now descended the shaky stairs and returned their keys to Madame. Frank had already paid the bill. Their suitcases were safely locked away in a storage room until it was time to put them into a taxi and go to the airport. There remained just enough time for lunch and a final drink in their favorite little outdoor café just around the corner.

Their café, Le Sélect, occupied one side of a little cobblestoned square surrounded by buildings of five or six stories. It was an oasis of tranquillity hidden away from the rush and clamor of the city. There were about a dozen tables, most of them occupied by other tourists who had also heard about the charms of this secret little place. The headwaiter in black tuxedo and small waxed mustache was able to seat them at once. After enjoying a white wine whose modesty was well deserved, they ordered the prix-fixe lunch: salad, steak, *pommes frites*, and pâté, the immemorial repast of the Gallic people. And just to make it perfect, a strolling accordionist in a striped shirt played the sort of minor-keyed lament that keeps French popular music a local phenomenon.

Frank Blackwell felt peace pervade his soul. He was experiencing a sensation of connection with an ancient, more gracious world.

He took Claire's hand. "Honey," he said. "I'm sorry. I'm not absolutely sure what I did wrong, but I'm really sorry I hurt you."

Claire's smile could still move him. "I'm sorry, too," she said. "Sometimes I don't know what gets into me."

They heard music coming faintly from the street beyond their cobblestoned square. It grew louder, the sound of guitars and mandolins and singing voices. Then the musicians came into the restaurant court-yard. There were four of them. They were dressed in medieval costumes of hose and puffed trousers and long cloaks. They were singing what Blackwell took to be an old ballad. They were young men, sallow-skinned and bearded, not particularly musical.

"Who are those guys?" Claire asked.

"Students, probably," Blackwell said, knowledge-able from his previous visits to the City of Light. "They sing in cafés and people give them change."

"What language are they singing in?"

Blackwell didn't recognize it. It wasn't English or French or German. He knew there were a lot of South American students in Paris, but the songs weren't in Spanish, either.

They finished the song, and Frank fumbled in

his pocket for some change. Then one of the students flipped back his cloak, revealing a small automatic weapon slung across his chest.

Blackwell just had time to remark to Claire, "You know, that guy's got a gun!" Then the students had thrown back their cloaks, unslung automatic weapons, and begun firing into the café.

Frank grabbed Claire's hand and pulled her down under the table. Bullets hailed through the courtyard, ricocheted off the gray-black cobblestones, and pocked the dark yellow walls of the surrounding buildings. A cry of outrage and alarm came from the diners as they scrambled for cover. Bodies began to tumble around like leaves pummeled in an autumn storm. The accordionist dived for the entrance of the café, and just made it, a swarm of bullets following him like steel-jacketed hornets spawned in a munitions factory. The accordion, left behind, let out a long quavering high-pitched scream as bullets smashed into it.

Blackwell, crouching behind an overturned table, felt Claire's hand pulled violently out of his grasp. He looked around shaking with fear and anger, and saw her lying five feet away. She seemed to have come apart. The part of her with the plaid skirt had been torn away from the part of her with the nice little jacket from Bloomingdale's. He stared at her. For a little while he could make out five distinct circles of blood, where she must have been struck. But then the bloodstains widened and ran into one another.

The courtyard was blue with cordite fumes. Eight other people also seemed to be dead. The students, or whatever they were, had left. They were a Balkan terrorist group demonstrating for a free Montenegro. They had picked Le Sélect to make their point because they thought (erroneously) that the Yugoslavian ambassador and his wife were having lunch there. They were caught two days later by the French police, in Cagnes-sur-Mer on the Mediterranean, where they were trying to catch a boat to Africa. In the ensuing gun battle, all four men were killed.

Blackwell learned that later. Now he just stood around, miraculously untouched, carnage on all sides of him, Claire's shoulder bag in his lap.

The police arrived and took statements. Photographers arrived and took pictures. Reporters arrived and recorded for posterity the banal indignation of the survivors. A hearse arrived and attendants took away the dead, after zipping each of them into his or her own bodybag. Claire had to go with them, of course.

A man from the American embassy arrived, expressed his regrets, and gave Frank his card. He said he would let Frank make all necessary arrangements to repatriate Claire's remains. Blackwell thanked him.

Finally they were all gone. All except Blackwell, who didn't really have any place to go and was more or less at loose ends.

The waiter had also survived. He asked Frank if he would like a drink.

Frank did, but couldn't think what to order. The waiter suggested champagne, the best in the house. It wasn't every day that your life gets shattered, your wife killed, and the course of your destiny changed forever.

When the waiter went to get it, Frank tried to open Claire's bag. His passport and traveler's checks were in there, along with the plane tickets.

The bag wouldn't open. Frank saw that two of Claire's severed fingers were still clutched tightly around the clasp.

He looked around. No one was watching.

He tugged at the fingers, gently at first, then with more force. The fingers opened suddenly and fell to the cobblestones.

The waiter was returning with his drink.

Frank found a handkerchief, wrapped it around the fingers, put them in his pocket. Then he started to cry.

The waiter put his hand on Blackwell's shoulder.

"Courage," he said.

Blackwell said to the waiter, his voice choked, "Somebody's going to pay for this."

It's what victims always say.

2 • • • • •

Frank Blackwell left Paris with his wife's ashes in a simple metal urn.

At De Gaulle, the security people wouldn't let the urn go through until Blackwell showed them a certificate from the Prefecture of Police attesting that the urn contained the remains of a victim, not the means of making others.

Blackwell flew into Newark International, and had a three-hour wait for the bus to South Lake, New Jersey. The trip to South Lake took another three hours. Blackwell stared out the window the whole time looking at nothing, which is to say, New Jersey.

Claire's parents were waiting for him at the hardware store which also served as the town's bus station. Mr. Niestrom was a natty little man who always carried a bamboo walking stick. This was the first time Frank had ever seen him in a suit. Mr. Niestrom's eyes were red. Mrs. Niestrom was a large woman with a faint mustache. She started crying as soon as she saw Frank.

"Who did it, Frank?" Mr. Niestrom said, as soon as they were in the car.

"Four young men. They were Montenegrin terrorists."

"That's what they said on the news," Mr. Niestrom said. "But I missed it when they explained what a fucking Montenegrin was."

"It's a country," Blackwell said. "Or it was a country once. I'm not too sure."

"One of them nigger countries?"

"No, it's in the Balkans. Between Albania and Yugoslavia. Or was. If it ever was an independent country, I mean."

"I just thought, what with a name like that, they'd be Africans."

"Well, it's a natural mistake," Blackwell said. He was having a little trouble handling Claire's father's mixture of sincere grief and sincere bigotry. But, as Claire had told him, you get to choose your wife, but not your in-laws.

"They killed the bastards, though," Mr. Niestrom said. "That's right, isn't it, Frank?"

"Yes, that's right."

"In a way, I'm sorry they done that. You know why, Frank?"

"No, Mr. Niestrom. Tell me why," Frank said, for what he hoped would be the last time in his life.

"Because I woulda wanted to kill them myself."

Claire had told him how the old man used to beat her when she was a kid. Mrs. Niestrom would hold Claire's glasses and the old man would beat her with a strap. For being bad, whatever that was. "You wouldn't believe that skinny little man could be so strong." And she'd laughed.

"She was my baby," Mrs. Niestrom said, and burst into tears.

Dinner that evening was subdued.

Frank stayed over at a motel on the edge of town so he could attend the special service for Claire at the Lutheran church to which she was no longer affiliated.

He couldn't help but feel a little resentful that it was Claire who had gotten killed and left him to bury her and deal with her parents and then try to figure out what to do with the rest of his life. Rather than the other way around.

Not that he wasn't glad to be alive.

Basically.

3 • • • • •

After the church service Blackwell rented a car at the local Rent-a-Wreck agency and started back to New York. As he turned onto Route 101, he remembered Minska's Tavern, just down the highway between the Mobil Flying A and the Ethan Allen furniture outlet. He used to go there a lot with Claire. He decided to have a last one for old times' sake.

Minska looked the same as ever, a big man, hairy up to his ears, bald after that. He had a handlebar mustache and a potbelly the size and shape of a bowling ball, but not the color, since Minska was of Polish descent. He had pop eyes and walked with his feet splayed out like Donald Duck. He was a funny-looking man, and people in South Lake used to take him lightly, even contemptuously, until the night he and Tommy Trambelli, who they used to call Tommy Trouble, had it out.

That was two years ago. Tommy Trouble was a warehouseman at the big Sears five miles east of Netcong on Route 123, and that night he had just won the annual Garibaldi Day arm-wrestling contest at Saddle River and was pretty filled with himself. He started making fun of Minska. Imitated his walk. Imitated his sort of slow Slavic way of pronouncing things.

Minska just smiled and continued polishing glasses.

If you live in New Jersey, you have to get used to loudmouthed warehousemen.

Then Tommy insulted the kielbasa sausage Minska always served, cut into sections and speared with toothpicks decorated with red frizzled cellophane, for the delectation of clients during Happy Hour. Minska got a little red in the face but let it pass.

Then Tommy asked Minska when his ancestors had come down out of the trees, was it before or after World War II? And Minska sighed and wiped his big red hands on his apron and said, in his mild high-pitched voice, "All right, Tommy, you say enough now, so just shut up before I breaka your face."

Tommy was a little taller than average, but he looked short because he was muscled like a goddam bear or something. He was a weightlifter, too, a karate black belt, and had been a dandy shortstop in high school.

He said, "Well, Minska, if you'd ast me nice maybe I'd of eased up on you. But you can't give me no orders, know what I mean, man?"

"I'm giving you an order," Minska said. "Get out of my tavern and don't come back until you can keep a civil tongue in your head."

Tommy put down his Miller High Life, straightened his Bruce Springsteen T-shirt, and said, "You gonna make me?"

"Yeah," Minska said, "that's what I'm going to do."

He took off his apron and came out from behind the bar. Everyone moved away to give them plenty of room. Incongruously, the jukebox was playing Cole Porter's "Begin the Beguine," a super golden oldie.

Tommy danced up and down on his toes and came in jabbing. He had been a pretty good middleweight in reform school and might have gone somewhere as a pro if it hadn't been for trouble with the Mafia. But that is no part of this story.

Minska stood flatfooted, arms dangling at his sides. Tommy jabbed hard at his forehead and Minska took the punch and stepped forward, coming down hard on Tommy's instep with his big yellow Georgia boots. Tommy made a noise somewhere between a scream and a grunt and doubled over, and Minska clubbed him across the back of the neck with both hands interlaced and that was the end of the fight.

Some people wondered after that where Minska got those moves. There was one story that he'd been a sumo wrestler in Warsaw's Japanese quarter, but everybody knew the communists don't permit professional wrestling. Joe Duggan, who drove an eighteen-wheeler for Exxon, set everybody straight. He had seen Minska's name and photo in an old issue of *Soldier of Fortune* magazine. Minska had been chosen as Mercenary of the Month.

So what was he doing now, operating a tavern in South Lake, New Jersey? Nobody knew. Nobody asked.

Blackwell, driven by an alcoholic impulse rarely encountered in so normally abstemious a man, threw back his second double bourbon, controlled his desire to retch, and ordered another. Minska brought over the bottle, but didn't pour.

"Listen, Frank," he said, his voice slightly hoarse and vaguely Polish, "none of my business, but this doing you no good."

"It's not supposed to," Blackwell said.

"I'm sorry about Claire. Permit me to express my sincere regret, Frank."

"Thank you, Minska," Blackwell said.

The two men stood together comfortably for a while. Late-afternoon sunlight, rendered gelid by the admixture of New Jersey industrial by-products, poured golden light filled with radioactive dust motes through the mahogany interior of the bar.

"Is it true that you were a mercenary?" Blackwell said.

"Yah," Minska said. "Is true, I was mercenary."

"What was it like?"

"I enjoyed many aspects of it. But after a while it became difficult to justify the overview. We had to kill too many people who were just sort of standing around in the wrong place. So I decided to go into the tavern business in New Jersey and cultivate a Polish accent."

"Tell me something," Blackwell said. "How do I go about joining the mercenaries?"

"What you want to do that for, Frank?"

"Sometimes events conspire to produce in you a confusion of emotions that can only be satisfied by the taking of human life. I want to kill somebody, Minska."

Minska put his thick-fingered Slavic hand onto Blackwell's forearm. "Frank, believe me, there's a better way."

"What way is that, Minska?"

Just then two fat customers came in the door, followed by a thin customer.

Minska pushed a pad and a stub of pencil to Blackwell. "Put down you phone number, Frank. Somebody will get in touch."

4 • • • • •

The Hunters got in touch with Frank Black-well one rainy evening in November, when, under leaden skies, New Yorkers slouched onward toward Thanksgiving and the holiday madness that lay ahead. Soon it would be the season to be jolly, and for this reason alone people up and down the five boroughs were contemplating drink, drugs, or suicide, anything to escape the necessity of pretending there was any redeeming feature whatsoever to their miserable lives.

Frank was in his apartment on Greenwich Avenue eating Stouffer's baked bimbos and wishing Claire were here making him her specialty, ham steak with drophead biscuits. It's always the little things you miss, the giggles in the bathroom, the tears in the bedroom, and the special things you used to do, like going down to Chinatown once a year just for the heck of it.

Frank was brooding about this when the downstairs door buzzer rang. He looked at it suspiciously. People just didn't ring your doorbell at nine in the evening in New York unless they telephoned first so you wouldn't be alarmed.

He pressed the communications button. "Who is it?"

"Pizza delivery."

Blackwell couldn't remember ordering a pizza. "What kind is it?"

"Double cheese with pepperoni."

Blackwell frowned. The recent Pizza Delivery Murders had given a sinister connotation to that once popular order.

"Go away. I didn't order any pizza."

"Are you sure?"

"I'm almost sure, and that's good enough for me."

"Actually," the voice said. "I'm not a pizza man at all. That was a joke. I have an important message for you concerning an offer which may not be repeated."

"Send me a letter," Blackwell said, and returned to his dinner.

Half an hour passed. Frank finished his dessert of Borden's Instant Plopovers filled with marmalade made from genuine chemicals. He put the indestructible plastic containers into the garbage can for their eventual trip to the garbage mountain on Staten Island. He was ready to settle down to an evening of television.

No sooner was he installed on his sagging couch than he heard a sound from his small bedroom. It was difficult to know what it was, but it could have been the noise a steel bar makes when it snaps the lock on the iron grille of a bedroom window.

Blackwell stood up and looked around wildly for a weapon. He found a breadknife with a plastic handle and a patented edge. It would have to do. He wished he had bought the home-defense grenade kit he had seen during the recent sale at the Counterinsurgency Boutique. He made his way quietly over the mounds of newspapers that Claire used to change once a month to the darkened bedroom.

A man stepped out of the shadows. "Hello," he

said merrily. "I'm Simmons. Minska tells me you're interested in killing people."

He brushed past Blackwell and went into the living room and sat down. Blackwell hesitated for a moment, then put the knife down on a bureau and followed.

"How did you get in?" Frank asked him.

Simmons held up a pair of bell-shaped devices with straps and buckles and pressure-release valves. Blackwell recognized them as Clompers, suction devices designed to take a grip on the porous surfaces of most of New York's older buildings.

"A silly trick, really," Simmons said. "But useful for getting the attention of prospective clients."

Simmons was a slightly built man in his mid-forties. He wore rimless glasses, had gray-blond hair cut in an unbecoming brush, a little pug nose, and colorless eyebrows. He was a wimpy-looking guy in a gray business suit, not too new, not too well cut. He was the sort of man the essence of whose presence is absence. He looked so harmless that Blackwell was sure he had to be dangerous.

"First," Simmons said, "let me express my profound regret over the shocking murder of your wife."

"If you're a recruiter for mercenaries," Blackwell said, "you've got a complicated way of going about it."

"Oh, I have nothing to do with mercenaries," Simmons said. "I work for quite a different organization. It's something more dangerous than mercenary work. And more satisfying. If you can dig it—pardon the expression."

"Spell it out for me," Blackwell asked.

"The people I work for, Mr. Blackwell, hunt the biggest, baddest, meanest animal of all. Man himself. I'm from the Hunters."

*   *   *

Blackwell had heard of the Hunt. Who had not? The secret organization, irrational but appealing, had been making headlines in recent years, staging their Hunts in cities around the nation, often under the eyes of the police, who seemed unwilling or unable to do anything about it. The Hunt was popular among Americans, and there was talk that it might soon become legal, especially since Congress had recently passed the Suicide Normalization Act decriminalizing self-murder, as long as it was performed in one's own house and didn't violate the civil rights of other people.

"I don't know," Blackwell said. "The idea of going out and killing some stranger—well, it's appealing, in a way, but what has that got to do with Claire?"

"Quite a lot," Simmons said. "The normal basis for the Hunt is random selection among volunteers. But at present, due to an imbalance in our Hunter/Victim ratio, and also as a social service, we have expanded our program to include the elimination of assassins and terrorists and professional hitmen with friends in high places. They are the sort of people responsible for your wife's death."

"But the people who killed Claire are dead."

"The ones who actually pulled the triggers, yes. But what about the permanent class of people behind them, middle- and upper-level managers of political and economic murderers?"

"Do you mean I could Hunt the people who set up the Paris atrocity?"

"Not the same people, but people engaged in similar work. The Hunt is not designed for personal revenge."

Blackwell thought about it and found the idea appealing. He really did want to kill somebody, and it would be satisfying to kill the sort of person who had been responsible for Claire's death. Of course, there was no doubt a possibility that he could get killed himself. But there was no sense being negative this early into the thing.

"Well," Blackwell said, "I'm interested. I'd like to hear more."

"Good!" Simmons said. "Why don't you come to one of our secret meetings, get a feel for how things work, then make up your mind?"

"All right," Blackwell said. "Where do I go?"

"Oh, I can't tell you that," Simmons said with a smile. "Secret, you know. But we'll call you in a day or two and we'll set it up."

"Okay," Blackwell said. "I suppose you have my office number, too?"

"Of course." He shook Blackwell's hand. "It's been a pleasure."

Blackwell walked with Simmons to the front door and unlocked the bolts. Simmons disappeared into the night.

The adventure had begun.

5 • • • • •

Frank Blackwell was working that fateful fall as a free-lance book editor for Elsinore Press, a small publisher with offices on 23rd Street near 7th Avenue. Simmons called him at work two days later and gave him an address on 60th Street near 9th Avenue. Blackwell agreed to be there at eight o'clock.

Frank took the subway to Columbus Circle. Since he was early he stopped at the Cajun Fast Food Place on 58th and Broadway for a cup of coffee and a shrimpburger jambalaya with a side of bayou fries. Then he walked to the address he had been given.

It was a large new apartment building. As Blackwell hesitated outside it, a car door opened nearby and a tall, dark man with long sideburns and wearing a chauffeur's uniform got out.

"Mr. Blackwell?"

"Yes?"

"I'm the chauffeur. Mr. Simmons sent me. Please get in the car."

"Simmons told me to come here," Blackwell said, indicating the building.

"Oh, that was just the first step, sir. Security, you know. I am to take you the rest of the way."

"The rest of the way where?"

"To where Mr. Simmons and the others are expecting you."

Blackwell was starting to get a little annoyed. "Is this mystification really necessary?"

The chauffeur smiled regretfully. "Well, we *are* a secret organization, sir."

"Oh, all right," Blackwell said, getting into the back of the stretch Cadillac. "Where are we going?"

"Jersey," the chauffeur said, moving his neck unpleasantly back and forth within its cylinder of starched white collar.

"Jesus," Blackwell said.

The limo slid away from the curb with well-bred speed, and the chauffeur began the first of a series of maneuvers that would bring them to the Lincoln Tunnel.

In early August 1827, John Farley Todd, a nephew of the recently deceased Thomas Jefferson, was rambling in the Appalachians, a popular pastime in those days. His journey had begun at Monticello, New York, from which point he had trended southward with a pack and walking stick. Todd had crossed the ridge of Kittatiny Mountain, whose crest runs to the Delaware Water Gap, and was continuing through the tangled hills above Franklin.

At some point, he found a fault line between two folded hills. At the point where the two rock masses met, concealed beneath heavy vegetation, Todd, an ardent amateur geologist and popular young society lawyer from Camden, New Jersey, found a narrow fissure leading down into the bowls of the earth. He noted the discovery in his journal, not failing to liken it to Coleridge's "deep romantic chasm which slanted down the green hill athwart a cedarn cover," though in this case the cover was pine and pin oak. This journal is the most precious possession of the Hunt Archives.

Todd descended through slanting beams of motey sunshine which grew ever dimmer as he came into what he described as "the cyclopean gloom of these vast depths."

He found himself at last in a vast cavern far below the earth's surface. The cavern's walls were lit by luminescent lichen, which gave off a "blue-green light, lambent and shadowless."

Looking around him in awe, Todd remembered the last words of his illustrious uncle, Thomas Jefferson, spoken just a week before his death on July 4, 1826:

"This country is presently in a prosperous mood, my boy, and seems a not unreasonable place in which to live. But the blessing of good government is a delicate bloom oft tramped in the race to profits. A day may come when men of goodwill may find themselves in need of a refuge in which to plot against unfairness and tyranny from abroad, or unctuous devilishness from within. If you should ever run across such a place, by all means secure it for the future when its need will be made manifest."

The exact meaning of Jefferson's words, and even their accuracy, has been argued with vehemence. But it is certain that Todd purchased the tract within which the entrance to the secret cavern was concealed.

His descendant, Edward Todd Jackson, an independently wealthy big-game hunter of liberal views, leased it to the best cause he knew, the Hunt Corporation.

Frank Blackwell learned all of this much later. For now, he only knew that the limousine drove for what seemed like forever through the nondescript suburbs of New Jersey, and then through rural countryside less interesting than the suburbs, and then along a dirt track for several bumpy miles, coming at last to what looked like the entrance of an abandoned mine shaft.

Serious-looking men came out of the nearby guard shack and conferred with the chauffeur in whispers. They looked at Blackwell for a long time. Then one of them gave Blackwell a plastic card marked VISITOR—RELIABILITY UNKNOWN. It had a pin on the other side so he could attach it to his jacket. "You'll need this down there," he said.

"You're thorough," Blackwell said, just to be able to say something.

"We have to be," the guard said, as he always did when a visitor commented on his thoroughness.

He led Blackwell inside the mine shaft to an old French-type elevator with open wire cage door and Art Deco ironwork. The guard motioned him to get in.

"I don't know which button to push," Blackwell said, in a desperate attempt at levity.

"Don't worry," the guard said. "I'll push your button."

His simple words had a sinister effect as the elevator plunged downward into the depths of the earth.

6 • • • • •

The elevator came to a smooth stop. The door slid open automatically. Blackwell stepped out into a vast vaulted room carved out of the granitic bedrock. Indirect lighting recessed behind natural convolutions in the stone gave the place the look of the movie set for *Tarzan Finds the Lost City of Ophir*.

Directly ahead of him there was a receptionist seated at a glass-and-chrome desk. She was icily beautiful, and she surveyed Blackwell with the hauteur natural to clerical workers in secret underground facilities. She took his pass, held it up to the light to check the watermarks, then called somebody up on the telephone and held a short discussion.

"You may go through," she said, and directed Blackwell through a door into a paneled corridor with old Currier & Ives prints on the walls.

At the end of the corridor there was an armed guard, and he too checked Blackwell's pass before letting him through into another corridor.

This next corridor was filled with secretaries walking back and forth with their hands full of papers, talking about romance, and with busy executives followed by administrative assistants drinking black coffee and talking on cellular telephones.

At the end of this corridor a guard wearing a green uniform with gold flashings stamped Blackwell's pass and directed him to a door marked NO ENTRY.

The door slid open when he approached, and closed behind him after he had stepped inside. Across the room from him was Mr. Simmons, sitting behind a walnut desk, wearing a pale yellow suit open to reveal a paisley vest.

"Ah, Blackwell, pleasant journey I hope?" He came around the desk and shook Blackwell warmly by the hand. "I know it's a little dreary having the company headquarters so far from New York, but we were unable to locate a suitable cavern under Manhattan. Do sit down. Drink? Martini. Very dry. Twist, no olive. Beefeater's. Got it right, haven't I?" He winked roguishly. "Moneypenny!" The receptionist looked in the door. "Two martinis, one very special one for our friend here James Bond."

"His name is Blackwell," the receptionist said in a voice that implied that she had been through this charade before.

"Oh, heavens, of course!" Simmons said, pressing his fingertips to his forehead. "It's just a temporary aberration. Of course you're Blackwell. Don't know what I was thinking about."

"It comes from continual fantasizing," the receptionist said. "I've told you that before."

"Yes, Doris. Now go back to your desk."

Doris made a face and flounced back to her desk, the door sliding shut behind her. Blackwell and Simmons stood and regarded the door for a while.

"Stunner, isn't she?" Simmons said. "The high hard buns of youth. Making a fool of myself, I suppose. Never mind. I let her think I'm a bit crazy. I hope you won't mention this to anyone."

"Never," Blackwell said.

"Come right this way and let me show you around."

He led Blackwell into a large room filled with rows

of men and women sitting in front of computers. "This is the Computer Room, of course, the heart of the operation. Lucy, if you'll excuse me—?"

The young lady whom he had addressed, who had crisp auburn curls and a cheerful face devoid of makeup, obediently vacated her seat at the console. Simmons slid in. His pudgy fingers danced on the keys, interrupting every now and then to seize the mouse and pull down a menu or some such operation—the machines all being Macintoshes, of course, since the company had seized ascendency in the computer field some years previously—and up came a variety of displays.

"This is our Informant Hot Line. We have a growing number of people who, while not willing or able to join the Hunt themselves, feel a moral obligation to supply us with information about likely candidates. And over here is the Running Master List of all Hunts currently active. It is updated hourly. And here are the data bases from which we select our Involuntary Victim List. That's the one you're interested in. The one with the death-squad people on it."

"That's the one." Blackwell said.

"No problem about that. We know all about everyone. We are able to tap into any data base we care to. We can get into police and government secret data. We even have our own list of the Fifty Worst Cases. That's on a worldwide basis, and our measurements for badness were developed for us by licensed semanticists working in conjunction with highly motivated programmers."

"You go to a lot of trouble," Blackwell said.

"Oh, it's big, Blackwell, it's very big. We're going to be legal someday, you know. We're going to be an institution known and respected throughout the world.

We're the founding fathers of a new order." Simmons looked for a moment, in his stern purity, like an idealized portrait of Marx, Lenin, and Engels standing on a cloud addressing the cheering sailors of the battleship *Potemkin*.

"But that's for the future. The question before us now is, do you think you can commit yourself to hunting down and killing one member of the professional killer class?"

"Oh, yes," Blackwell said. "No trouble. But tell me—just for my own information, I mean—is there really a professional killing class?"

"Oh, yes. Our sociologists have proved that since the beginning of recorded civilization, there have been people born every generation who combine a love of following orders with a taste for violence. This sort of person tends to put himself into positions in which he can kill his fellow man. Such people are useful to their rulers, because they will do anything, no matter how vile, as long as they are assured from time to time that it is all for the best in the long run. It doesn't take a lot to satisfy them intellectually, and many of them volunteer for special forces. It would be all right if they would confine themselves to killing each other. But they don't. We of the Hunt, though we are devoted to the ideal of Hunting in all its purity, recognize our social duty. It is one of this class whom you will Hunt, Mr. Blackwell, if you choose to stay with us."

"What must I do to join?"

"There are several requirements. You must drop out of regular life for the period of the Hunt. We can help you with that. But once you begin, you must see the Hunt through to the end."

"What happens to Hunters who drop out without completing their kills?"

"They tend to have nasty accidents," Mr. Simmons said. "It's best to be sure in the beginning. If you decide to join, we'll give you the best training available in this line of work. We'll give you a Spotter who'll help you set up the kill. We'll expedite your mission in every way short of doing it ourselves."

Blackwell said, "I'm just wondering, what sort of man becomes a Hunter?"

Simmons smiled gently. "Your true Hunter is an old-fashioned man trying to return to an individual-centered world. He is a sportsman who wants to play the most dangerous game. He is an existentialist locating himself in instantaneity. He is a child waving a sword. He is a man following an idea whose time has come. That is what a Hunter is, Mr. Blackwell."

"Is a Hunter also someone who wants to get even?"

"Yes, Mr. Blackwell."

"Then I want in."

7 • • • • •

After Blackwell left, to return to New York to make his arrangements to drop out long enough to kill his Victim, Simmons touched a button in the wall. A panel slid back, revealing an elevator. Simmons got in and went down to a lower level.

He went through a short passageway of undressed rock. A single naked light bulb guttered above a simple doorway. Simmons took off his shoes and stepped soundlessly into a small chamber, candlelit and as bare as a monk's cell.

At the far end of the room, an old man sat facing a blank wall in zazen fashion, his legs folded onto a square black cushion. He wore a simple homespun robe. He appeared to be frail, not well, perhaps; but his shoulders had an indomitable set.

Without turning his head, the old man said, "Good afternoon, Simmons."

"How'd you know it was me?" Simmons had seen the trick before, but he liked to encourage the Huntmaster's few remaining vanities.

The Huntmaster chuckled. "You walk very quietly, Simmons, more silently than a creep; but even no-sounds can be heard when the mind is quiet."

"What if my no-sounds really made no sound?"

"Then I'd know you by your smell."

"And if I eliminated that by encasing myself in a giant Baggie?"

"Then I'd know you by your aura."

"And if my aura were missing?"

"What is missing also leaves a trace."

Simmons grinned ruefully. The Huntmaster could always best him in these Hunt mondos.

"I came to report, sir, that I have signed that new Hunter we were discussing."

"Blackwell? Good."

"But I'm troubled," Simmons said.

"Indeed?"

"Following your orders, I have concealed from him our deeper purpose in enlisting him for the Hunt."

"The opposite of the truth is also true," the Huntmaster pointed out. He stood up in a single flowing movement, the dull brown robe swirling around him as if it were alive. The flickering candlelight softened the intellectual but determined lines of his face. He could be irritating sometimes, as Simmons knew only too well. But he was the driving inspiration behind the Hunt philosophy, the Thomas Aquinas or Rabbi Akiba of murder, the St. Francis of mayhem.

"Tea?" the Huntmaster inquired. Without waiting for an answer he crossed the room and stirred up the embers of a charcoal fire in a low iron brazier. Stooping, fanning the flames to life, the Huntmaster added a few sticks of kindling. When the fire had blazed up he swung over it an ancient copper kettle, suspended from an armature of jointed iron.

"Perhaps the Master will see fit to inform me at this time," Simmons said, "why it was so important to get this particular man into the Hunt."

"His importance is positional. His characteristics further a deeper plan. Let me give you an analogy. In chess, all the pawns are of equal value, is that not so?"

"Hai!" said Simmons.

"But it is not really so. One pawn move can unmask the attacking queen. Another pawn move can expose the shrinking king."

"So Blackwell sets up a potential in this particular situation which another Hunter wouldn't do?"

"That's true, but only as an analogy. Whichever pawn you use produces a singularity of result which is part of the nexus of the future. Blackwell's moves will predispose rather than set up certain moves from the other side."

"But won't this be dangerous for Blackwell?"

"Of course. But he too must serve the cause, if not willy, then nilly. The times have conspired to produce a need for him. America is in a period of rapid change. Laws decriminalizing all aspects of the drug business are now on the books. Suicide is no longer against the law. Murder has been officially condoned under an increasing number of circumstances. Legislation for the Hunt's legalization will be brought forward by our friends in Congress within the year. We are very near being able to go public, Simmons. And at this very stage of our development we must take certain risks in order to avoid others."

Simmons nodded, astonished as always by the old man's grasp of the situation. Not for nothing was the Huntmaster known as the Cardinal Mazarin of Massacre.

"Still," Simmons pointed out, "it's a bit hard on Blackwell, isn't it?"

The Huntmaster's look was at once gentle and unyielding. "He might come out of it alive. Stranger things have happened."

8 ••••••

Dropping out was easy for Blackwell to do. With Claire dead, no one gave a damn whether he lived or died. He had finished his last free-lance editing job, *The Junk Food Lover's Guide to Europe*. His editor, Marcia Gottshalk, was pleased, in her mild way, and told him to come around in a month or two, or perhaps a little longer, and they'd probably have something else for him. With the assistance of Hunt Covert Funds, Blackwell prepaid his rent six months in advance, packed a light suitcase, and, per instruction, took a Deltoid flight to Phoenix.

He was met at the airport by a taciturn man in a fawn-colored Stetson who led him to a battered pickup and drove him to the Hunt Training Facility in the Superstition Mountains of northern Arizona. He was assigned a cabin and a seat in the dining room. Clothing and equipment were issued to him. The next day his training began.

His first instructor was named McNab, and he was black, but he spoke with a heavy Scots accent. Perhaps he was putting Blackwell on. It was difficult to tell about some of the strange types who taught assassination and allied arts at the Superstition Mountain facility.

"You see, laddie," McNab told him, "in the killing business, it's usually not so simple as just walking up to Mr. Target and sticking a gun in his ear. And forget about that long-distance sniper's shot. It looks great in the movies, but in actual practice it's awkward to carry a high-powered rifle with zeroed-in scope around with you. And if you need to do your work out of the country, forget it. You wouldn't want to be caught with one of those things coming through customs, local sensibilities being what they are. In fact, forget about rifles altogether. For close-in work, you'll use a handgun, or one of those lethal toys our Development Section is always coming up with. But to my way of thinking, a walking stick is better than any handgun made, and an umbrella is better yet."

McNab was an expert in umbrella fighting.

"I'm not talking about a sword umbrella, mind. Too risky if you get caught. Too specialized. What I'm discussing here is a plain umbrella with a wood or bamboo shaft, though we have a model made of surgical steel that's the best of the lot. You can sharpen the point. And if the handle is rounded and weighted with lead, you've got a murder weapon at either end."

Six foot eight and black as the ace of spades, McNab demonstrated the basic moves: the feint in which you pretend to open the umbrella, the lunge for the target, the first riposte, the second riposte, the follow-up with the weighted handle. Blackwell practiced faithfully several times a day. He became proficient, though never got as good as McNab, who had spent a lifetime in rainy climates practicing his trade.

Houston James, a bald-headed mountain man with a red beard, gave a course in standard small arms.

"You can't let yourself depend on any particular weapon," he told Blackwell. "The successful assassin must depend on what comes to hand. And we don't have time to teach you the niceties of handgunning. It's enough for your purposes to be able to pick up any weapon that comes to hand and know how to load it, release the safety, and fire. It's easy to kill with a gun, but you'll have problems if you don't know how to get a round into the chamber if it's an automatic, or whether it fires on full cock or half cock, hammer up or hammer down. By the time you get out of this class, you'll be able to use any of these fifty-two commonly used handguns, rifles, and light machine guns.

In the unarmed combat class, the instructor, a small, grinning Gurkha from a village just outside of Katmandu, taught them one thing and one thing only. "As you will not be here long enough to learn karate or aikido, or the Tibetan mung-ho, which is superior to all other systems, I'm going to teach you just one thing. Go for the balls, gentlemen, the balls!"

The instructor went on to point out that the balls were an ideal target. "Forget about hitting a man on the jaw. You could break your fist that way. Forget about throwing him over your shoulder. You could put your back out. None of that stuff is any good at all unless you really know what you're doing with it. Attack the balls, gentlemen. And if your opponent is a woman, you can use the same technique by pretending she has balls."

In explosives class, Blackwell learned the fundamentals of bombs and detonators, but only the most basic basics. His instructor, a small, balding man with a soft Irish accent, told him, "There's no time to teach you how to make your own bombs, more's the pity. It's a beautiful art, but no one should attempt it except after years of apprenticeship with an expert. Too much chance of blowing yourself up. I'm going to show you how to use certain explosive devices which you may encounter in your travels."

None of the instructors thought very much of guns. One told his class, "They don't kill people nearly as fast or as efficiently as they're supposed to do. But the real difficulty is that every police department in the world is geared to detecting firearms, tracing their identification marks, locating powder marks on your hands, and so forth. You're playing into their strength when you use a gun.

"What are the best ways to kill a Victim? Poisons have some advantages, more disadvantages. We have some very fast-acting ones. Hit your man with a dart, stab him with a pin, blow powder in his face, he's done for. But so are you if something goes wrong. And something goes wrong more often than not.

"The important thing is to keep your eyes open, get close to your Victim, look for fortuitous accidents. Be determined, be alert, and above all, be sneaky."

9 • • • • •

After nearly six weeks, Simmons came to Blackwell's room. "How are you getting on?" he asked.

"I like it," Blackwell said. "I suppose that's the wrong attitude, but it's how I feel."

"No, it's the correct attitude. Don't be ashamed of enjoying killing, either the notion or the execution. We humans have a long past as hunters and killers. Much longer than as civilized beings. Do you feel all right about what you're going to do?"

"I suppose so," Blackwell said. "But I wish I could get on with it. It's difficult for me to believe I'm actually going to do this. Kill this man. I mean, yes, I know I'm going to, but I still don't completely believe it."

"Most of us have a deep-seated aversion to killing our own kind," Simmons said. "Although we do plenty of it despite the taboo. Still, it's the greatest single hurdle a Hunter must overcome."

"Do all Hunters get over it?"

"Some do, some don't. Some, despite the best will in the world, can't perform when the moment comes."

"What happens to them?"

"The Victim usually kills them."

"I think I'm going to be able to do it," Blackwell said.

"You're going to get your chance. We finally have your target set up for you. I have his dossier here.

He's a wealthy man, and well protected. Here, read this." He handed Blackwell a computer printout.

Alfonso Alberto Guzmán Torres was born in 1933 in a medium-sized city south of Managua. His father was an Armenian merchant with no social position but plenty of money. Young Alfonso was educated at good schools, and in 1949 when he was sixteen he entered the Nicaraguan Military Academy. He graduated in 1952 determined to make a career in police work. He went to Peru and for the next four years studied at the national Academy of the Civil Guard, taking many interesting courses not available at home.

Upon his return to Nicaragua he joined the police force in Managua and was assigned to the National Security command. His ability, cool ruthlessness, and political reliability were recognized and he was made commandant of the model prison in Managua. He reached the rank of colonel. In 1970 he married Doña Caterina López, of the famous López family with estates in La Flor and El Castillo, one of the fourteen families who counted in Nicaragua.

When his excellency the President of the Republic Anastasio Somoza fell from power in April 1979, Guzmán, Doña Caterina, and their three children escaped to Guatemala in a Nicaraguan air force cargo plane. In Guatemala City, Guzmán joined FRENICA (Frente Revolucionario Nicaragüense), one of the early contra groups, but soon switched to the more active FDN (Fuerza Democratica Nicaragüense—Nicaraguan Democratic Force), which became the main contra group to receive U.S. support. He took part in the unsuccessful Plan C, then was seconded to FAD (Fuerzas Armadas Democritas), and then to

FARAC (Fuerzas Armadas Anti-Communistas). His ability to tolerate the pain of others, together with his talent for small arms and conspiracy, made him an ideal death-squad leader.

He knew there was a certain stigma to his job, but he bore it like a man. Sending leftist pigs to Commie Heaven in the Indian villages of the Cordillera de Yolaina or in the corn fields around Bocay was not the job he would have chosen, but someone had to do it.

Guzmán was wounded in an FSLN ambush near Matagalpa. His second in command, his boyhood friend Emilio Salvador Aranda, got him across the Río Coco to Danlí in Honduras, and then the CIA flew him to a Miami hospital.

He brought Emilio to the States with him—one good turn deserved another. He also brought Tito, a hulking man, quite bright for a moron, who had been his sergeant at the model prison in Managua. And he didn't go back to Nicaragua: the FSLN had marked him for execution, put a price on his head, declared him a sadistic criminal rather than a soldier. He stayed in Miami, acquired American citizenship (easy with his good political record and his CIA contacts), and sent for his wife and children in early 1982.

In Miami, with the help of friends, and his wife's family's money, which had prudently been invested in Costa Rican coffee futures, he was able to get into the construction and shipping businesses.

He never gave up his old sideline of killing people, however. There were plenty of Nicaraguans in Miami with big noisy mouths which needed stopping, preferably with quick-setting cement. Guzmán, with the aid of a few of the boys, took care of these people. He also was a key figure in shipping arms to various right-wing groups throughout Central America.

"What am I supposed to do?" Blackwell asked. "Go to Miami and see if I can get him?"

Simmons shook his head. "Guzmán is well prepared for that sort of thing. It's been tried, with no luck at all. We're going to have to get you close to him."

"Maybe I could go up to the door and try to sell him an encyclopedia."

"He never answers the door. He's got people around him to run interference. He's got a huge house in South Miami protected by the most up-to-date alarm system in the world. He's got bodyguards, Dobermans, an electrified fence. Nobody gets near him unless he sends for them."

"Doesn't he ever go out?"

"Of course he does. He goes to jai alai, restaurants, sometimes to the Biscayne Club. But there's no pattern. He doesn't plan it ahead of time, nobody knows, he just calls up his bodyguards and goes. You can't set anything up when the pattern is as random as that."

"Well then, how do we get close to Guzmán?"

"That's what we're working on. They're quite a problem, you know, these old death-squad jocks. It's amazing how many friends and supporters they have, despite anything they've done. They're usually on good terms with local government and law-enforcement agencies. And they give generously to local charities."

"Makes it difficult," Blackwell said.

"And it's especially difficult in a county like Dade,

which is dominated by Miami. You've got a lot of people spread out over a hell of a lot of land. It's an enormous tropical slum. Aside from a few big buildings in the center near West Flagler and Biscayne, it's nothing but endless miles of one- and two-story buildings. There are dozens of little neighborhoods spread out from Homestead to North Miami Beach. Many of these neighborhoods are occupied by blacks or Hispanics. A stranger in these areas, especially an Anglo, sticks out like a sore thumb. And people throughout the Greater Miami Area are extremely suspicious. There's high unemployment and high crime. A lot of dope smuggling, trade in arms, and illegal aliens. A lot of murders. Every few days the police find a car in an irrigation ditch alongside some county road. When they pull the car out they find a corpse inside. By the time they get him to the morgue the land crabs have been at him and it's difficult to tell even how he died, much less who killed him."

"Too bad I'm not Hispanic," Blackwell said. "It would make this a little easier."

"It wouldn't help at all," Simmons said. "Not unless you were born and raised in the Miami milieu. Even if you were Hispanic, anyone could spot you as an outsider as soon as you opened your mouth. And then you'd be twice as suspect."

"You make it sound pretty discouraging," Blackwell said.

"I just wanted you to know the real situation. But we've faced problems as tough as this before. We just have to wait for the window of opportunity to open."

"What's that?"

"It's a term we use for the few hours or days in which a victim becomes vulnerable. It can come up pretty fast, so it's best to be ready for it. Better get back to your training. But be ready. When we need you, it's going to come pretty fast. I'm going to have you take the special course in Tropical Assassination and Evasion. It contains some techniques you'll find useful in the Miami area. And it will also provide you with something you'll need so as to not look too completely out of place."

"What's that?"

"A really good tan."

PART TWO

THE MAKING OF A VICTIM

10 • • • • •

While Frank Blackwell was doing his special training, events hundreds of miles away, in Honduras, were conspiring to make his Victim accessible to him. There, on a rocky ridge near the city of San Francisco de la Paz, two contra guards sat keeping watch on the main road, which wound over the flat, treeless horizon like a dusty, tapering black snake.

Behind them, the rebel camp of Miguelito and his Cobras sprawled across three treeless brown-and-tan hillsides overlooking the muddy Río Télica. In its gypsy haphazardness, the camp looked like a rag-pickers' convention in downtown Port-au-Prince. But though it lacked many amenities, the camp was convenient to Nicaragua just across the river, where the people continued to support a leftist regime despite the fact that this government was intolerable to American interests. That was a mistake the Nicaraguans were continuing to pay for.

The two men lounged at their ease, shirts unbuttoned to the waist and shoes unlaced, in the manner of guerrilla troops all over the world, especially those in tropical climates. It was a day of intense blue sky, with purple-bellied clouds sailing up from the Gulf of Mexico like Spanish galleons, bringing with them the crop-ripening rains, which were late this year, as they were most years.

One of the lookouts, a short, bearded, dynamic

little man named Valeriano, had been a student at the university in Silves, eighty miles upcountry from Managua. He had been studying Elizabethan literature when a contra conscription team broke into his dormitory and forcibly enlisted him in the army of the liberation. His friend Panfilo had been his roommate at the university and engaged to Valeriano's sister, Pilar. He, too, had been seized. Panfilo was the other guard on the ridge.

All that had happened twelve years ago. Now Panfilo stood with his shirt open, leaning over a ridge, smoking a Mexican Delicado cigarette and watching lazily as his friend Valeriano swept the gleaming black ribbon of road with battered 7×50 Zeiss binoculars.

Both men heard the scuffling sounds of feet behind them and turned warily, AK-47s at the ready. But it was only Jean-Claude, the cook, a short fat man wearing a white apron.

"How goes it at the camp?" Valeriano asked him.

"Terrible, terrible," Jean-Claude muttered. "I had to get away for a few minutes. I must get control of myself." He sat down on a rock. His hands were shaking. He stood up again immediately and began to pace.

"Take it easy, friend," Panfilo said. "I think you're hitting the stuff a little too hard, if you know what I mean."

"I only use it to stay alert," Jean-Claude said. "And besides, what can I do, everybody in the camp is high all the time, Miguelito keeps on passing it out. But I'm not having a drug fit. I'm just worried about the pig."

The two guards, both former university students, stared at the cook as if he had gone loco. "Are you referring to someone we know?" Panfilo asked.

Jean-Claude stared at them, perplexed. "I'm talking, of course, about the pig for the feast."

Panfilo and Valeriano both slapped their foreheads with the palms of their hands, a gesture recently imported into Nicaragua from Italy. The feast! Of course! Because the reason they were on the ridge was to watch for the arrival of Ramón de las Casas, the FSLN(C) representative from Miami. And of course there was a feast in his honor, and this man, Jean-Claude, had to be referring to the pig for the feast, the *lechón asado*, which is always served to visiting dignitaries wherever the Spanish language is spoken, even if they are vegetarians.

"But what is wrong with the pig?" Valeriano asked. "Is it not a nice pig?"

Jean-Claude gritted his teeth. These men irritated him, but at least they were educated, even if they did wear their shirts open to the waist. Not educated in the *French* sense of the word, of course, but not bad for Hispanics.

"The pig is perfectly nice. I selected it myself. The problem is that our guest is late. I *told* Miguelito he'd be late, because delegates are always late. I told him we should not put the pig on the spit until we saw the taxi from San Francisco de la Paz coming up the dusty diminishing black snake of the road. But of course I'm only a cook, and who ever heard of Commander Bandera Negra taking advice from a cook? Put it on now, quoth he—for *he* is the *comandante*, I a mere cook, although I do come from Bordeaux and used to work in the Holiday Inn there until the unpleasantness with the eleven-year-old Estonian girl forced me to emigrate."

"What did you do about the pig?" Valeriano asked.

Jean-Claude shrugged. "What could I do? Orders are orders. I put the pig on the spit."

"Well then, what's the trouble? Did you forget something from the recipe?"

Jean-Claude turned down his mouth in scorn. "Me? Omit some step from a recipe I myself invented, and which was featured only last month in *Gourmet*? No, I followed my usual routine, basted the piglet in maguey leaves steeped in tequila, stuffed it with herbs and spices and cornbread, rubbed it down with my own special preparation of herbs, oiled it with the last of the ultra virgin olive oil from Seville, and turned it over to the spit turners. They performed well, rotating the spit at the exact speed I set for them with my metronome and continuing without slackening until the pig was done to a glowing dark gold, the skin just bursting with savory juices, crisp on the outside and melting on the inside, the way *lechón asado* is meant to be."

"Any chance of saving a little for us?" Panfilo asked.

"You still don't understand," Jean-Claude said. "The pig is done to perfection *right now.* to leave it on the spit another ten minutes will scorch it and harden the tender meat within."

"Then take it off!" Panfilo cried.

"But then it will cool prematurely and I will have to serve cold meat covered with congealed white pigfat."

"Why don't you wrap it in aluminum foil?" Valeriano asked, grinning, since it was not his pig and he hadn't been invited to the feast.

"You know we have no such thing here," the cook said. "I wish I were back in the Tegucigalpa Hilton. If only there hadn't been that unpleasantness with the German tourist and her baby."

Valeriano had been scanning the road. He raised his hand imperiously. "Soft! Even now, he comes!"

A dust cloud had appeared at the farthest point of the tapering dusty black snake of the road. Soon it resolved itself into a speeding automobile. It was a dust-colored Plymouth, the taxi from San Francisco de la Paz.

"The feast is saved!" cried Jean-Claude. He rushed back to the contra camp.

"That's not all that's saved," Valeriano remarked to Panfilo. "Now the troops will be given the extra ration of Peruvian blueflake special that Miguelito promised them so they'd be bright-eyed and cheering when de las Casas arrived."

"And now the great man is here. Go, bid the soldiers snoot."

The two English majors exchanged a quiet smile, not really leaning into it, just tossing it back and forth slow and easy for a while. Then they put it away, wiped their noses, and went to report.

The Plymouth negotiated the boulder-strewn road lined with roughly hewn tree trunks, turned up the hillside, and swept into the camp with a flourish. The assembled troops, bright-eyed and bushy-tailed, cheered loudly, waving their caps and wiping their noses. A five piece mariachi band flown in from Tabasco struck up a rollicking huapango.

Out of the backseat stepped Ramón de las Casas, the liaison man for the FSLN(C), a group dedicated to retaking the Nicaraguan homeland and reinstating the policies of the late lamented Tacho Somoza and his Guardia Nacional, only this time with less leniency.

Casas wore a well-cut white suit and black string tie. With his long, finely molded face and wavy gray hair he looked like a cross between Bolívar and Saint Martin of the Fields.

Miguelito, the contra commander, the famous Comandante Bandera Negra himself, came forth to
greet him with a huge *abrazo*. Miguelito was a scruffy,
plump man with gap teeth and a crazy look in his
eyes. A *New York Times* stringer had described him as
a cross between Eli Wallach and Attila the Hun.

They went to Miguelito's tent. Casas lounged back
in a canvas chair while Miguelito filled little ornamental cups with grayish-white *chicha*.

"I hope the journey was not too fatiguing?"

"Not at all. And I hope you received the shipment
of women I sent you last month through our agent
in Guatemala City."

"They have been distributed among the troops,
who thank you, as do I."

"Were they all right?"

"Excellent. You have impeccable taste, Don
Ramón. . . ."

Miguelito's voice trailed away. Casas said, "What
was the matter with them? Not fat enough, eh? I
know, I know. But you can appreciate how difficult
it is to find decently upholstered whores who are
willing to travel. I keep on telling this to our agent in
Panama, Manchego de Quesadillo, but he just makes
excuses."

Through the open tent flap you could see the
mountains of the Sierra de Agaltá, colored deep
violet and edged in gold. The strident heat of the
tropics had faded from the sky. A few heavy drops
of rain began to fall.

"Goddammit," Miguelito said. "It looks like the
rains are coming early this year. And here we are in
these worn-out tents, camped out on this godforsaken
hillside with no movies and not even fat whores to
keep us company in the squalor and splendor of the

Central American night! Thank God the supply of pigs is holding out."

From outside came a cheerful, French-accented cry: "Peeg's ready! Come and git it!"

"A word with you before we join the festivities," Miguelito said. "I didn't ask you all this way just for a pig feast, Ramón, even though it is in your honor. I asked you to come to tell you that we are ready at last."

Casas sucked in his breath sharply.

"You mean *ready* ready?"

Miguelito's eyelids flickered, a minimalist gesture of affirmation all the more powerful because of its diminutiveness.

"How many men do you have?"

"I was able to hire nearly four thousand seasoned fighting men from Flavian Estes, Comandante Gato Azul. He has decided to retire from the guerrilla business and take up watercoloring in Fiesole, so I took every soldier he had. I got a very good rate, but even so I had to use all of my CIA maintainance funds, plus the little we had socked away in the brigade kitty from the pillage of Tumbuqú last fall."

"Four thousand is good," Casas said, "but still . . ."

"Wait, there's more. I concluded firm agreements with the leaders of other insurgent bands. They're getting bored sitting around and have agreed to attack when I do. Ramón, we can do it this time!"

"Miguelito, I say it with admiration, you have been very busy."

Miguelito smiled. "Now you see why they used to call me El Exigente before I became Comandante Bandera Negra. Ramón, we could go all the way! I'll cross the river at Dos Ojetes, outflank the Virgen Gorda Line, smash through the leper battalion at Dolces de Muerte, link up with Jorge Encendadora and his Purple Caterpillars outside of Morena de Churri."

"Brilliant!" cried Casas. "And then what?"

"Then we switch to Plan Honcho Azul, which you will remember we discussed last year at the guerrilla convention in Jamaica when I had the pleasure of meeting your beautiful girlfriend and her strange little brother. Then, with all forces united, we disperse in order to converge at Point Taco Enchilada for the final push on Managua."

"It's absolutely genius-level," Casas said. "I really mean that, Miguelito. No wonder they call you the Napoleon of Bocachica Province."

"There's just one thing I need."

"I know. Fat whores."

"They would be extremely useful, of course. But what I was referring to was weapons."

Casas' face fell. "That's always the hard part. Especially in the quantities you will require."

"And we could really use some antiaircraft guns. And a couple of tanks wouldn't be a bad idea."

"Hey, take it easy. Next thing you'll be asking for full field packs and boots for everybody."

"And a couple of medical teams would be helpful. The men expect it, you know."

"Miguelito, I'd love to accommodate you, but it isn't just up to me. The Revolutionary Council of National Freedom in Exile has to vote on it. But the organization doesn't have that kind of money." Casas made a quick calculation. "Hombre, you're talking upwards of twenty million dollars. That ain't chicken liver, if you'll excuse the *norteamericanismo*."

Miguelito's face slumped into a despairing rictus of discouragement. "I knew it would come to this. *Ineffectualismo*, that's what it is."

Casas said, "Miguelito, we've been friends a long

time. This is Ramón you're talking to, you know what I mean, baby? Look, really now, will your boys fight?"

"Will they fight?" Miguelito said, his voice hard and flat in the deep purple of the tranquil Central American twilight. "I've got them wired and ready to kill. It's the drugs, you see. We were lucky enough to stumble across a party of cocaine smugglers trekking across the mountains disguised as a *National Geographic* photographic team. I confiscated their stash and I've been passing it out to the men ever since. Those boys are *ready*. You notice all those chopped-down trees on your way up here? The lads did that, grinding their teeth and lunging with their bayonets. We're running out of forest and you're asking me will they fight! They'll fight, Ramón, all I have to do is keep them cranked up on product so they'll advance with the proper spirit when the time comes. But the attack has to be soon, before I run out and they either crash or kill each other, and probably me and the whores, too."

"Listen," Ramón said, "if I were able to supply you with the things you need—"

"Then you would be the next president!" Miguelito cried. "I am not a political man. All I want for myself is to be Commander in Chief of the Armed Forces in Perpetuity."

"Well," Casas said, "I will admit it's a temptation."

"Come on, Ramón, let's either do it or let's give up and take what we've got and run to Spain. I'm getting sick of sitting in these hills trying to keep thousands of childlike soldiers amused without even fat whores to help."

Just then Jean-Claude burst into the tent, his eyes rolling, his hair wild.

"My dear fellow," Miguelito said to his disturbed chef, "what is the matter?"

"I don't like to interrupt you, Comandante Bandera Negra," Jean-Claude said, choking out his words like a Japanese actor interpreting a big scene, "but unless you and your guest come to dinner immediately I am going to resign and join a contra band which cares about its food."

"No need for that," Miguelito said, laughing. "We're going to eat the pig, every bit of it, eh, Ramón?"

"Yes, and that's not all we're going to eat," Casas said.

"You mean it?" Miguelito said.

Their eyes met with the look of hawks. Casas gave a husky nod and clasped Miguelito around the shoulder.

"All right, my friend," he said. "We're going to go for it."

11 • • • • •

Ramón de las Casas left the contra camp shortly after the suckling pig feast, not forgetting to compliment Jean-Claude, who recalled his graceful words in the foreword to his cookbook, *The Contra Gourmet*, published some years later.

The tall, classically handsome FSLN(C) representative told his taxi driver to take him to San Leandro airport in Tegucigalpa. There were few passengers around, just a lot of soldiers with bayonetted rifles and a few Indian women with children huddled in the corners wrapped in brightly colored blankets. Casas drank coffee and cognac in the VIP lounge until morning. Then he boarded the seven-o'clock Pan Am flight to Guatemala City. He arrived just minutes before the beginning of the weekly meeting of the ruling council of the Free Republican Nicaraguan Liberty Democratic Party, the FSLN(C).

The delegates met in the opal suite of the Hotel Huespedes, a gaudy Spanish building built in a neoplateresque style with Gaudíesque overtones. They were small men, many of them, wearing white shirts, discreet ties, and dark suits. All had well-shined shoes and some of them carried worn briefcases. Quite a few of them wore glasses.

Under the slow-moving overhead fans, shirt sleeves rolled up, voice hoarse with earnestness, Casas presented the case of offering Nicaragua as collateral for a loan big enough to finance the guns for Miguelito's contras for a single throw of the dice, winner take all.

There were objections. What about the United States? asked Patricio Seguidiya, the watery-eyed minister-in-exile for foreign affairs, with his club foot and his habit of knocking over water glasses. Seguidiya pointed out that recent opinion polls showed 79 percent of the American electorate was against active support for the contras or anyone else, and that an important 87 percent couldn't tell one Central American country from another and nearly 82 percent didn't want to know.

"Don't worry about the Americans," Casas said. "They are aware that our party is the only one in favor of enslaving our economy to their giant corporations. They'll come around."

"But how can we be sure of their attitude?" Seguidiya asked.

Garcilaso Vegas stood up. He was a slender young delegate from Choyotepe.

"I believe I can set your minds to rest on that point," Vegas said. "I am the CIA mole in your organization, and I have been authorized to say that we'll back you all the way if you ever actually get off your backsides and get this war going."

A vote was taken. It was agreed unanimously that de las Casas should approach the Bahamas Corporation, an international financing company for shady weapons deals, and ask for twenty-five million dollars—because there had to be something left over for the delegates—in exchange for a chattel mortgage on Nicaragua.

12 • • • • •

The Bahamas Corporation was a curious anomaly of the stressful years as civilization moved toward the millennium. It was a private corporation made up of idealistic men and women, most of them scientists of the first rank, dedicated to pursuing the most worthwhile goals in illegal ways. The need for such an organization had become apparent as scientists grew more and more concerned about the threats to humanity posed by insensate industrialization. These people perceived that even if nuclear war continued to be averted, in another fifty or hundred years the planet would still end up unfit for anything but cockroaches and electric eels. And although visionaries had proposed leaving the earth in great starships, it looked like it would all be over before the starships ever got built.

Population growth and the multifarious forms of pollution: the human animal was overgrazing his range. The human animal had destroyed everything in sight, killed off the other big animals, used up millions of years of deposits of fresh water, oil, coal, minerals. Fragile ecosystems had been pushed to the limit, some of them beyond recovery. The death of the earth was undramatic, but it was happening, and fast. And the governments continued to squabble and defend their various economic, religious, and social doctrines. The wealth of nations large and small was bled into the continuing effort to increase the size, ingenuity, and ferocity of the armed forces. The humans were killer ants, devoting all their time to breeding more powerful mandibles.

Something had to be done immediately to preserve and maintain the great interlocking global system of ecosystems that sustained all life upon the earth. Only by managing the entire earth as a single unit could the basis of life continue beyond the next century or two.

But twentieth-century civilization was locked into its self-destructive groove. Nothing could be officially done until the various threats became much more threatening. But by the time that stage had been reached, it would probably be too late to do anything.

Key thinkers in a number of disciplines recognized that if the earth was to be saved from man's folly, it would have to be done outside the usual channels.

It would, in fact, have to be done illegally.

Ad hoc groups of concerned scientists met, discussed the problem. The key to the earth's salvation lay in funding. Only with enormous amounts of money could global problems be tackled.

Where would the millions, the billions, perhaps the trillions of dollars come from? Neither government nor the private sector was going to come up with anything like the amounts needed.

The Bahamas Corporation was formed to address that problem.

Only one enterprise recommended itself for the creation of large amounts of wealth in a hurry. That, of course, was crime.

It was a bitter thing for the scientists to realize. Many of them had not even cheated on their income taxes, and had no dealings with the law other than the usual drunken-driving citations. Nevertheless, they faced up to the situation, and accepted the terrible logic that drove law-abiding men of highly idealistic nature to engage in crime.

It wasn't right; but it was a better option than letting the politicians blow up or pollute the entire world, as their current plans seemed to call for.

Thus was born the Bahamas Corporation, made up of scientists from all nations concerned with the preservation of the earth as habitat for all human beings, not just those with certain skin colors, religions, or political or economic beliefs.

They went into international loan sharking on the highest levels, aided by patriotic Mafia and Tong leaders who were willing to lend their time and expertise to this enterprise.

They soon found they didn't need advice from anyone. For men who could master particle physics, or chromophratography, or soil diffusion by the crystal impact method, learning how to make shady deals for great profits wasn't too difficult.

One special study group studied ideal drug requirements from the point of view of users, and came up with a hybrid marijuana twenty to forty times more powerful than anything ever smoked before. Superverde, as it was called, had very little odor and looked just like bean sprouts. A little went a long way. The Bahamas Corporation was well on its way to capturing the world marijuana market.

Their Supercoke didn't hurt the nose. One line kept you going for hours. But best of all, Supercoke could be woven into a light cloth, and with the admixture of silicate gel, turned into a hard paste that could be coated on the undersides of cars and scraped off at the other end.

But these developments were still in the future. At this time, the Bahamas Corporation was making most of its money through loans. And a very interesting proposition had just come to its Western Hemisphere offices in Outer Cay, 158 miles northeast of Nassau in the Bahamas.

Within the Main Boardroom the windows were shuttered, and the slanting afternoon sun turned the richly appointed room into a dazzle of brass and walnut. The air conditioners huffed silently away, making the room cold enough for the dark blue wool company blazers which the board members wore.

Dr. Alois Dahl called the meeting to order. Educated in the Netherlands, he had received his Ph.D. from the University of Utrecht. Two years later he joined the Stanford Linear Accelerator Center at Stanford University. After four years at Berkeley, he went to the University of Michigan, where he was appointed Edward T. Flynn Professor of Physics. The previous year, he had been selected by the Scientists' Secret Board in Geneva to take command of the Bahamas Research Institute following the still-unexplained death of Hans Castorp, the previous incumbent. Dahl was a large blond man, with a reddened freckled skin that refused to tan.

"The main item on our agenda," Chairman Dahl said, "is the request from Ramón de las Casas of the FSLN(C) for a loan of twenty-five million dollars for the purpose of acquiring arms and overthrowing the present government of Nicaragua. I believe you have all studied the proposition?"

The five men at the meeting nodded or made meaningless doodles on their scratch pads.

"I would appreciate your comments," Dahl said.

Isao Yakitori, who came from the U.S. National Geodetic Survey, where he had been studying very-long-baseline interferometry, spoke up. "The proposed loan is extremely insecure. Casas wants this money to finance his gun deal. But how many weapons have these people gotten in the past, and what have they got to show for it? Their proposal that they repay us in five years by levying a fifty percent peace tax on the population of Nicaragua sounds fine, but we have no way of making them comply in the unlikely event that they ever do come to power."

"I think my colleague overstates the negative side of the case," said Eduardo Macidelli, professor of chemistry and biochemistry at the University of Colorado in Boulder. "The risk is great, but so is the return; two hundred percent over five years is not bad."

"*If* they get into power," Yakitori said.

Chairman Dahl said, "Can't you see that the return of our principal is secure no matter what happens? A proviso of our agreement with the FSLN(C) is that their man in Miami, Alfonso Guzmán, will buy the arms from Yitzhak Framijian, our gun dealer in Miami. When Guzmán pays Framijian for the arms, we get back our money. In effect, we'll have done an arms deal with ourselves, repaying our twenty-five million plus our profit on the arms. We don't stand to lose even if the FSLN(C) doesn't succeed."

"Breaking even is not the point of being in business," said Mark Clancy, an associate professor of anatomy and zoology at the University of Illinois at Urbana. "And what about this man of theirs, this Guzmán? Is he reliable?"

"In financial matters, he is a man of honor, like so many of these old death-squad jocks," Macidelli said.

"I don't like mixing in politics this way," Yakitori said. "Politicians are unreliable. Why don't we simply stick with financing terrorist operations? It's done pretty well for us so far."

"I think some of you are missing an important point," said Dahl. "We can gain from this operation, not only monetarily, but by the prestige we will achieve in international circles by having financed a government overthrow. We have to move with the times. Financing terrorists has about reached its limit as a growth industry. It is time to move into something new. Financing revolutions is definitely the wave of the future for private capital. If we needed a reminder, we have the recent home-office memo to that effect."

"I suppose it's all right," Yakitori said. "I only hope this decision won't come to haunt you later on."

"My sentiments exactly," Macidelli said, with a wolfish grin.

Dahl smiled, but he felt a twinge of fear. A chairman of the Bahamas Corporation was allowed very few mistakes. Even a single one was overdoing it. A mistake could lead to rapid demotion. And at the Bahamas Corporation, the only place a chairman of the board could go was straight down into the blackness of Tongue of the Ocean clad in a concrete overcoat. The home office still hadn't figured out how an organization devoted to illegality could devise a legal succession of power.

The vote was taken and passed unanimously to grant the FSLN(C) the loan requested, subject to the agreed-upon stipulations. Chairman Dahl went back to his quarters.

13 • • • • •

As soon as he received a coded cable telling him that the sum of twenty million dollars had been deposited to his Panamanian account, Alfonso Guzmán reached for a Montecristo Special Select No. 1 cigar from his cedar-lined humidor. As he lighted it, he felt regret that there was no cigar expensive enough to celebrate so large a coup. Twenty million! Of course, he would have to pay out most of it to get the arms from Framijian, and another million or so would go to various friends, officials, expediters, and others. Still, he expected to come out of it with a clear profit. Not bad for an Armenian merchant's son.

He savored the moment for as long as possible, sitting back in the leather-covered Barcalounger in his big white den on the second floor of his rambling pink house in South Miami. Then it was time to get on with business. He punched a number into his telephone.

"Mr. Blake? So happy to get you in. I have a matter to discuss with you. An extremely urgent matter."

Blake's flat voice came through tinnily: "Urgent for whom, Alfonso?"

"For us both, my friend. The realization of a great dream we both share. A dream involving the aspirations of both our great nations. A dream which also happily will mean considerable profit for everyone concerned."

"That's great, Al," Blake's voice came, heavy with irony. "But why bother calling me? Why don't you just take out an announcement in the *Miami Herald*?"

"This is a secure line," Guzmán said.

"How the hell do you know?"

"Because you told me," Guzmán said, feeling a little chastised. Blake always made him feel small and greasy and stupid. He hated Blake.

"And if I told you there's a pot of gold in the middle of the Orange Bowl, would you believe that, too?"

"Blake, I'm sorry."

"I don't know what kind of shit you've been smoking," Blake said. "You sound all weirded out to me. You really got something to talk to me about or is this another of your 'Flying down to Rio' fantasies?"

"This is important," Guzmán said. "Believe me, Blake."

"All right," Blake said. "I'll listen to your song and dance. Meet me tonight at the Dania jai alai. There'll be a ticket for you at the box office."

"Look," Guzmán said, "couldn't we meet here at my house? I've been trying to not go out too much, you know, ever since that incident last month with the crazy Colombian with the machete."

"Don't go all paranoid on me, Al," Blake said. "You wanna talk to me, meet me tonight at the jai alai. Over and out, baby."

Blake hung up.

Guzmán put down the phone. He took a silk hand-kerchief out of his pocket and wiped his forehead. If there was one thing he would have liked for Christmas, it was Blake's head on a platter, with an apple in its mouth, surrounded by steaming yucca, Central American style. And Blake was the one man he mustn't, couldn't, kill.

Still, maybe he could arrange an accident . . .

No, forget it.

Still . . .

He got up. One talk with Blake and all the pleasure of a certain two point five mil profit had gone down the tubes.

He snapped on the intercom. "Tito!"

Tito Herrera had been just outside in the reception room. He hurried in when the boss called.

Tito was a huge man, a mestizo from San Juan del Norte, a former sergeant of Guzmán's from the days when Guzmán had been commander of the model prison in Managua. Tito had a dark, dour face, creased and knife-scarred. He had a collection of dried ears which were considered the best in Miami in terms of variety of types, colors, and lobe styles. He had an old mother living in Panama City to whom he was devoted. Aside from that, Guzmán considered him barely human. But he was useful, the best bodyguard Guzmán had ever had.

"We're going to the Dania jai alai tonight," he told Tito. "We'll take the Lamborghini."

"OK, boss, consider it done," Tito said. He spoke good English from spending most of his time watching gangster movies on the VCR. He went to the door, hesitated.

"What is it?"

"None of my business, boss, but is this really a good idea? You know what I mean."

"I know what you mean. Just be alert. Now go get the car."

Almost a month ago Guzmán had been upstairs in

his den watching *Casablanca* on the VCR. The explosion was a distant heavy thud which might have been mistaken for an earth tremor. The floor shook briefly and the twenty-seven-inch television blinked twice before rearranging itself electronically.

Don Alfonso had put the movie on hold, gone to a small chest made of exotic tropical hardwoods, taken out a 9mm Browning, and checked the clip. He waited a few more moments to see if there would be another explosion. Then he went downstairs.

The laundry room wasn't a pretty sight. The laundress, poor old Tia Teresa, and a week's supply of shirts were plastered across the walls like a design for a freehand surrealistic barber pole. It was unpleasant even for a former commandant of the model prison in Managua.

He had gone to the living room. There he found his wife curled up into a large black ball in the chrome butterfly chair having hysterics.

Moments later, Juanito, Guzmán's twenty-four-year-old nephew, had come bounding in, yawning and scratching his curly head. He had been sleeping in a deck chair by the pool on the other side of the house and the explosion had awakened him.

"All right," Guzmán said, "we've had an unpleasant incident. Let's pull ourselves together. Juanito, call Cielo de Corazón Mortuary and have them pick up Teresita, then call the Trans-Caribbean Employment Agency and get me another laundress. And then call the plumbers. The sprinklers are off."

"Sprinklers?" Juanito said, smiling his uncertain smile.

"The bomb must have damaged the water pipes. The lawn sprinklers are off. You can see for yourself. Ten thousand dollars' worth of ornamentals which Gil & Eddy Florists put in just last month will be ruined. You'll find the number in the office."

Juanito went to the telephone in the office adjoining the living room. Guzman's wife, Doña Caterina, pulled herself together and rose shakily from the chair. "We must have masses said for the poor woman's soul."

Don Guzmán, remembering his movie, said, "Tell the priests to round up the usual prayers."

"What?" Doña Caterina asked. She was a tall, gaunt, white-faced woman with a regal bearing. She seemed to be modeled on one of the Spanish queens, Isabella la Católica, or, more likely, Juana la Loca.

"Nothing, my dear, just a little joke," Guzmán told her. He couldn't afford to alienate her entirely, or at least not openly. Not while she held the bearer bonds that were the keystone of his business ventures.

He had carried it off with style, no doubt of that. But it had shaken him all the same. And he still didn't know who had planted the bomb, or how it had been put into his laundry. There were so many people who would like to off him. He had redoubled his precautions, and had sent Tito out to take care of a few of the likelier suspects. And he had started staying home a lot more.

But that damned Blake and his jai alai. Well, if he brought this off, Guzmán swore he'd never leave his house again. They'd have to dive-bomb him if they wanted to kill him.

14 • • • • •

Guzmán, with Tito driving, turned off U.S.
1 onto Dania Beach Boulevard, then into the Dania
Jai Alai Fronton, a block long and illuminated like a
cruise ship. Tito gave the car to valet parking and
they went inside. Guzmán had considered arriving
early enough to have dinner in the clubhouse: he
was partial to the *zuppa di cozze*, mussels steamed
open in olive oil, with garlic, basil, parsley, and
chopped tomatoes, served in a soup tureen. But it
was late and he went directly to the reserved seats.
Everything was going nicely until the attendant asked
for his ticket, which Guzmán had forgotten to pick
up at the box office. When Guzmán couldn't produce it the attendant said he'd have to leave.

The attendant should have known better than to
hassle Alfonso Guzmán, even if he was new on the
job. Even if he didn't know who Guzmán was, he
should have been able to figure out something by
the way the man carried himself. If that wasn't
enough, there was Tito walking two steps behind
him like a Hispanic golem. That should have told
him something. So when Guzmán lifted the velvet
rope off its little brass hook and walked into the
block of reserved seats right down in front, the attendant should have figured he belonged there and
not have started a fuss.

Guzmán started laughing at the guy, and the attendant asked him what was so funny, and Guzmán told him he would look really interesting smiling with two mouths. Before the guy could even figure out what that meant there was Tito looming over him, about seven feet tall and thick and broad and ugly.

"This guy bothering you, boss?" Tito asked.

All of this in low voices, almost whispers, standing beside the reserved seats, Guzmán stocky and serene in his light alpaca topcoat and Tito with his shoulders bursting out of his white Miami Dolphins windbreaker and the attendant ready to shit his pants because he suddenly realized he was in trouble but he didn't know yet he wasn't important enough to kill.

Fear is the finest compliment to machismo, and Guzmán was content. "Just go away," he said, and took his seat.

He sat for a while watching the action. He was right on the edge of the cancha, 178 feet long, the long wall of the three-walled court. The Basques, with red plastic helmets and white slacks, tennis shoes, and team numbers on their colored T-shirts, saluted with their cestas and the round began.

There were four Cubans in the next block of reserved seats. They were betting quinielas, and one of them, barrel-chested with black curly hair, slapped his friend over the head with a folded program whenever his team made some progress. There was a fair-sized audience for off-season, mostly Anglos cheering the numbers they were betting on. "Come on, number two!" The players' names were in the booklet, but they were unfamiliar Basque names—Gorricho, Urreta, Larrusca, Assis III, Chaz. It was easier to cheer for the numbers. Guzmán decided to try for a trifecta on the next event, just to keep it interesting, and then Blake slid into an empty seat beside him.

Blake was small and sharp-featured and he had close-cropped sandy hair, what there was left of it. He wore light gray tropical worsted slacks, thin brown alligator belt, Dacron maroon-and-royal-blue plaid jacket, and white Saks loafers with little tassels.

It was too hot even for a tropical-weight jacket, but Blake wore his to conceal his gun, a flat, snub-nosed .32, not much stopping power but useful in face-to-face situations. He carried it in a chamois shoulder holster.

Blake's partner, Angelo Coelli, was six foot three and large for his height. He had a broad mournful olive face above a white guayabera shirt. No jacket: his flat, snub-nosed .32 was strapped to his ankle, just inside his Sand Boot.

"Well, how you doing, buddy?" Blake asked. Coelli took a seat in the row behind, beside Tito. The two men grunted at each other.

"My friend," Guzmán said, "it is good to see you."

"I'll bet," Blake said. He looked up at the announcement board and saw that the fifth contest was just ending. "Who do you like in the sixth?"

Guzmán didn't really give a damn about jai alai. He was a Miami Dolphins fan. But he made a pretense of studying the program. "Two and five," he said at last. "Goitterez is in great form this year, and Braça is the best backcourt man in the business."

"Bet 'em to win?"

"I would suggest a quiniela."

Blake twisted around in his seat. "Put a couple of bucks on it for me, will you, Angelo? And take Tito with you and buy him a drink."

Tito shook his head. "I stay here."

Coelli looked at Blake. Blake shrugged. Coelli went off to make the bet.

"So, buddy," Blake said, "how you been keepin'? How's the señora?"

"Very well," Guzmán said. He didn't inquire about Blake's family. He had no idea if the man had one. Did cockroaches have families?

"And to what," Blake asked, "do I owe the honor of meeting with you in this palace of sport?"

"A project of ours has finally come to pass," Guzmán said.

"Run that by me again in English, OK?"

"Miguelito is ready."

"Which Miguelito is that?" Blake asked. "The one in El Yunque or the one in San Francisco de la Paz?"

"The one in San Francisco, in Honduras. The one they call Commander Bandera Negra."

"I remember him," Blake said. "He was at the contra convention in Jamaica last year, right? Little man with big ideas?"

"Miguelito has absorbed fighters from three different groups. He's got five thousand trained men, and cooperation promised from the other groups. The FSLN(C) is behind him. He is ready to march on Santa Clara within the month, before the rainy season."

On the jai alai court, the new teams came out for the sixth game. Coelli came back from the betting windows and gave Blake two five-dollar tickets.

"What were the odds?" Blake asked.

"Three to one."

"Not so great," Blake said. "Still, maybe Al here knows something. So Miguelito's ready to roll? That's fine. I hope he's keeping the station informed."

"Of course. But there is a problem."

"Always problems," Blake said philosophically.

"Weapons. Ammo."

"Always the same problems."

"With respect, it's different this time. But this time he's ready to fight and win. This time, Blake, we could take it all, especially with Angel de Goyo's troops concentrated on the Guatemalan border."

Blake looked interested. "You know about that, huh?"

"I, too, have my sources."

"What does Miguelito need?"

"Guns and ammo for five thousand troops."

Blake whistled softly. "You're talking a lot of bucks, amigo."

Cheering from the crowd. In the court, all the pairs had been eliminated but two. One of the pairs was the pair Blake had bet on. He turned and watched the final round with interest. The pelota blasted against the back wall. "Nice *rebote*," Blake said. The opponent made a weak return. The front-court man made a classic two-wall kill. His opponent climbed the mesh trying to save the point, but it was impossible.

"Beautiful!" Blake said. He handed Coelli the tickets. "Collect that for me, would you, Angelo?" He turned to Guzmán. "You know your jai alai, amigo."

"I know my guerrillas, too. Miguelito is a winner."

"And he wants to buy weapons through you?"

Guzmán nodded.

"Lot of money for that much stuff."

"They say they have it. I'm not worried about it. But I wanted to clear the transaction with you."

"Well, tell you what," Blake said. "You go ahead and make your arrangements. Call Framijian—he'll handle it for you as usual. We'll expect your usual contribution to the CIA emergency fund before final delivery is made."

"Thanks, Mr. Blake!"

"Oh, hell, anything for the cause," Blake said.

15 ••••••

Yitzhak Framijian was a short, dark, powerfully built man of forty-seven. He was an Israeli, a sabra born and raised on a kibbutz near Eilat. He had been in the gun-smuggling business since childhood. His father had been an active supplier of arms to the fledgling Irgun and Hagganah forces at the time of Liberation. When the elder Framijian was killed in a terrorist attack at a crossroads near the Gaza Strip, Framijian had taken over the business.

For many years the new nation's need for arms had guaranteed Framijian a healthy income. But in the years following the Six-Day War the need for imported arms slackened. Israel was building its own arms and munitions factories and was becoming an important supplier to the world.

With his livelihood draining away as new small-arms plants came into existence on the outskirts of Haifa and Tel Aviv, Framijian emigrated to the United States.

He found that a good man with contacts all over Africa, Europe, and the Near East could do well for himself in America. He settled in Miami, pursued his contacts, and operated, if not legally, at least with the tacit consent of agencies such as the CIA, which found him useful to front arms sales to clients who were not supposed by law to receive them. His success brought him to the attention of the Bahamas

Corporation. Framijian preferred operating on his own, but they made him an offer he couldn't refuse, accompanied by a threat he couldn't ignore. He made more money with Bahamas, but it took some of the fun out of it. Still, Framijian always had known he'd have to grow up one day.

Guns sold by Framijian were used to repress Haitians, Dominicans, Chileans, Argentinians, and many others. Weapons supplied by Framijian were prominent in the unsuccessful Bay of Pigs operation against Castro. Some of Framijian's guns may have been used by the PLO against Israeli nationals. It was impossible to know for sure where a gun was going to end up. Weapons were like money—they circulated everywhere. Framijian knew that he was not to be blamed for how his weapons were used. No more than the owner of a shoe store in Munich in the 1930s, who sold a pair of jackboots to a customer, could be blamed if the customer used them to kick an old Jew to death in an alleyway.

He got a call from Guzmán on a Friday. Not an observant Jew, Framijian was eating a takeout order of blackened stone crab chow mein from Louisiana Wong, Coconut Grove's newest Cajun-Chinese restaurant, and watching *Friday Night at the Movies* on TV.

The two men had done business together for years. After the usual exchange of pleasantries, Guzmán mentioned that he was catering a banquet in about two weeks. He wanted Framijian to supply the fruit.

Framijian owned a fruit import and export business. It gave him some cover, and provided a useful way to talk about guns without actually mentioning them.

"How many guests will you have?"

"About five thousand."

Framijian gave a low whistle of surprise. This was going to be one of the biggest orders he had ever filled.

"So many?" he said. "It's going to be expensive."

"I know. I'm just catering it. My client wants the best."

That meant new guns, not old stock from the Vietnam War.

"I suppose," Framijian said, "you'll want an apple apiece for each guest?" An apple stood for an M-16 battle rifle or its equivalent.

"Yes, and some extras in case anyone is still hungry. Let's say six thousand apples."

"OK," Framijian said. "I suppose you'll be wanting grapes, too?" This referred to ammunition, each grape standing for two hundred rounds of the appropriate ammunition.

"Five grapes for each apple." A thousand rounds. "And two pomegranates per guest." Twenty hand grenades.

"All right, Mr. Guzmán. It's big, but no problem. That will come to . . ." He made a calculation. "About twenty dollars a guest."

When discussing money, they habitually dropped a couple of zeroes. Framijian was talking about two thousand dollars per armed soldier, coming to twelve million dollars.

"That is acceptable," Guzmán said. "How soon can you arrange delivery?"

"Give me two days, Mr. Guzmán. Call me the day after tomorrow, in the evening."

16 • • • • •

While Guzmán was talking to Framijian, his curly-headed nephew, Juanito, was sitting in his own room on the far side of the Pink Palace, monitoring his uncle's conversation through a telephone bug. The bug was connected to the very good Sony tape recorder Juanito used expressly for this purpose. He had been taping Guzmán's conversations for several months, but without getting anything of interest: Uncle Alfonso was a cautious man. But this time he was setting up a deal, and information about that was worth something to the right people.

Juanito had his reasons for this unfamilial behavior.

Beneath his smooth brow, downy cheek, and ingenuous eye, Juanito had all the problems of a man of position without the income.

You think it's easy to be the nephew of the wealthiest Nicaraguan in South Miami? That just shows how much you know about it. You probably also think it's wonderful to have as your girlfriend Thalia Suárez, Miss Teen Latino Queen of South Dade, cute and perky-breasted and saucy-assed and still in her last year at Miami High School, and already she'd had a walk-on in *Miami Vice* in the episode where Sonny poses as the reincarnation of an Inca prince to get to the bottom of a Mogambo operation that's fleecing poor folks in Hialeah.

Sure, it sounded good—nephew of the big man—

but being Guzmán's nephew didn't pay a salary, and where was a man to get the money he needed to take out his girlfriend and uphold his status among his peers on SW 8th Street in Little Havana?

And it wasn't as if Juanito didn't work. He did plenty of work, and it was all for his uncle. Guzmán usually had a couple of South and Central American buddies staying over at all times. He had these pals of his, the old Pistol Petes from the Guardia Nacional, who came over two, three times a week to drink his booze and stay for dinner. At those times the hospitality flowed, but it didn't just happen by magic. Somebody had to tell the cooks how much food to make, somebody had to tell the maids how many rooms to make up, somebody had to repark the cars so there'd be room for other cars, somebody had to take care of all the rest of the details. Somebody had to head up the operation, and that someone was not going to be Emilio. Emilio was an adviser, and advisers weren't permitted by their union to do anything but sit around in their overcoats and look menacing. And Guzmán's wife, Donã Caterina, wasn't going to play the hostess; forget it, she'd turned her blank white face away from worldly matters, spent all her time with priests and nuns. And it couldn't be Tito, because Tito was the bodyguard and a well-known killer and you couldn't expect a man with the finest collection of dried ears in greater Miami and maybe all of Florida to call Bender & Sons and order five dozen of their kasha varnishkas to be delivered by six that evening. That left Juanito, and he did it all. He was indispensable.

But only Juanito knew he was indispensable. Uncle Al just thought he was useful. He'd slip Juanito a hundred every week or so and think he was being real generous. Like he was doing him a favor. But there Juanito was, handling the petty cash and writing checks on the household account for the caterers, the garage people, the gardeners, the grocery people, and he was just twenty-five years old and he had no future except as Uncle Al's flunky.

It was Bender who got him on the take. Bender of Bender & Sons Caterers, seventy-eight years old, bald as a billiard ball, walked with two sticks, spoke broken English, and he ran everything; his two sons were just there to relay his orders to the help.

Bender ran into Juanito one day when he was down on Alton Road at the A&Z Wine Merchants checking out the new vintages for Uncle Al. Asked Juanito can he buy him a drink, he's got a little business to discuss, so they went into Ruggiero's near Jefferson and Lincoln Mall and Bender lost no time getting to it.

"We used to be your caterers," Bender said, "but now it's Vachensky all the time. I got no complaint, it's a free country, you can take your business where you like, but I'd just like to know, is there anything we did to displease you?"

Well he might ask, because Uncle Al Guzmán was a freak for Jewish food, what they call a maven, a caterer's dream, he dropped a couple hundred or more a week on Romanian pastrami, kasha, chicken in the pot, fricassee, pickles, and that was just for the household, that was not even counting the big parties every month or so.

"I don't think it was anything special, Mr. Bender," Juanito told him. "You're in South Beach and Vachensky Brothers is in Miami and they're a little faster getting the stuff to our house."

"You want fast? I can give you fast," Bender said. "Our delivery service has improved since I bought the new vans, and I got me a bunch of schvartzes who are driving fools. Our food is the same unsurpassed quality as it has been for twenty-seven years, and, although I don't like to say anything against a business competitor, Vachensky Brothers is well known on the beach for selling drek which isn't even truly kosher because they've got a rabbi on the payroll and he's Reform and doesn't even believe in kasruth. Maybe you don't know about that all stuff, Juanito, but your uncle, who is a connoisseur of Jewish cuisine, he cares."

"I'll take it up with him sometime," Juanito said.

"Does he really care which caterer you use?" Bender asked.

"No, he leaves it up to me."

"Look," Bender said, "since you are such a special customer, and since we are trying to introduce our Jewish specialities to the Latin community, I can offer you a special discount. Ten percent off everything. How does that sound?"

"Very nice," Juanito said, not too enthusiastic.

"The discount." Bender said, "wouldn't be reflected in the bills we send. The bill would be for the usual amount. What we'd do, you'd come by the main office on Arthur Godfrey Road once a week or whenever you like, and we'd give you the rebates in cash."

"That's convenient," Juanito said. "And I could bring the receipt to my uncle."

Bender shrugged. "Why bother doing such a thing? The discount is for you, personally. Our secret, just between you and me. I wouldn't want it to get around that I was giving you a discount. You know how Jews are—they hear somebody's getting a discount, immediately they want one, too. I wouldn't even want your uncle to know about it. And why should he? You're the one doing the buying and paying the bills. No, I'd just give the money to you, ten, let's say fifteen percent of whatever you spend with us, you wouldn't tell, I wouldn't tell, everybody would be happy."

"All except Vachensky," Juanito said.

"Vachensky deserves it for selling treif food to goyim who don't know the real thing. Don't worry about Vachensky. But that does remind me—just as a sign of my good intentions, I would be very pleased if you'd let me pay you an advance, a sort of a bonus so you'll know old man Bender ain't talking through his keister."

And he snapped out two crisp hundred-dollar bills and put them into Juanito's hand, and then he put his other hand over it and that was that.

Bender opened Juanito's eyes. He learned there were plenty of people who wanted to keep Uncle Al's business. And there were a lot of new people who wanted to get in on it. Juanito never had to say a word directly. Or at the most, "I've been thinking of placing my orders somewhere else." Pretty soon he had a really nice supplement to his salary.

But it wasn't enough. It's funny how as soon as you make more, you need more to support your new status. There had to be some other way of making money off Uncle Al. It was just a question of finding it.

So Juanito had been very interested when the little man from up north bought him a drink at the Café des Artes on South Beach and told him he was willing to pay very good money for information about Uncle Al. All Juanito had to do was install a bug, which came complete with easy-to-follow instructions in Spanish and English, and plug it into the beautiful Sony recorder which the little man was going to give him.

Juanito had agreed. That had been two months

ago. He had phoned several times, giving the man little bits of not very important data about changes in Guzmán's household. The little man sent cash, in hundred-dollar bills, to Juanito's post office box in Coral Gables. And the little man had said that he'd pay a lot better when he got something that really interested him.

This phone call was just the sort of thing the little man wanted to hear about.

Juanito went out that evening to the Source in Coconut Grove, one of his favorite spots. There was a phone booth in the rear. Juanito dialed collect to a number in New Jersey, and spoke for several minutes.

17 •••••

The man with the gun was dressed from head to foot in black commando clothing. A hood pulled tight around a black wool watchcap framed his face. He was holding a small Skoda .22 automatic, deadly at close range, leveled at Blackwell's stomach. He was standing about three feet from Blackwell, and he bounced up and down on black-sneakered feet.

"Come on, sucker," he said. "Go for it."

"I'm really not in the mood for this," Blackwell said, turning away.

"Face me, you bastard!" the man said, taking a step forward.

As his weight went onto his left, leading foot, Blackwell whirled. His left hand, stiffened into a hand-ax position, slashed down hard on the inner wrist of the man's gun hand. The gunman tried to continue his movement, evidently planning to turn completely around and bring the gun into play. Blackwell moved with the gunman's turn and turned into it, locking the man's right wrist under his left arm.

"All right," the gunman said. "That'll do." He and Blackwell disengaged. "Nice move," he said. "You do a pretty good frontal handgun disarm. You ever play baseball?"

"Left field," Blackwell said. "But I wasn't very good."

"Basketball would have been better. Those boys really understand a quick pivot. But you did fine."

"What about if the gun had been loaded? What about if you'd been really trying to shoot me?"

"Oh, I would have gotten you, of course," the instructor said. "But remember, I know what move you're going to make, because I just taught it to you. Against someone else, you'll have an element of surprise. Or at least we hope so. OK, time I turned you over to Skelly for your advanced icepick techniques."

They were on a karate practice mat set on a platform on a broad field. There were low ranch buildings nearby. Misty mountains framed the far distance. A lone buzzard wheeled slowly through the sky. To the left was a high-speed driving track. Here Blackwell had mastered the bootlegger's turn and the moonshiner's turn, and had gotten a passing grade in Crashing Barriers. Just past that was the artificial lake where he had practiced high-speed hydroplane racing and water skiing. Next to the lake was the Edged and Pointed Weapons Studio. He began to walk toward it.

A jeep came speeding from the main lodge and stopped beside him. At the wheel was Fritz, one of the junior umbrella-fighting instructors.

"Get in. Simmons wants to see you."

Simmons was in his office in the main lodge, impeccably dressed, as usual. He had on a paisley smoking jacket. His narrow black silk tie was perfectly knotted. He was sitting in one of the Queen Anne wing chairs, and there was another man sitting beside him, a big man with a tough, lumpy, ugly, good-natured face.

"Minska!"

"How ya doing, Frank?" Minska said.

"What are you doing here?"

Minska grinned. "I used to work here."

"You told me you didn't have anything to do with the Hunters."

"Well, of course I told you that. I lied."

"So what are you doing here now?"

"After you left I got to thinking. I started to think maybe you could use a good backup man. And frankly, I was getting a little bored. So I volunteered to be your Spotter. If you want me, that is."

"He's the best in the business," Simmons said.

"I know that without you telling me," Blackwell said. "I'd really like for you to be my Spotter, Minska."

"Good, then that's settled," Simmons said. "You can congratulate yourselves about it later. Right now I need to lay out the plan for you. There's not much time. You have to catch a flight out of Newark at eleven a.m. tomorrow morning."

"What's the rush?" Blackwell said. "I've been doing push-ups here for six weeks, and suddenly I have to leave on one night's notice?"

"You remember the window of opportunity I spoke about? It just opened up. It's not going to stay open very long."

"So this is it," Blackwell said.

Simmons nodded. "Still up for it?"

"I feel a little funny," Blackwell said, "but yes, if you can get me close to this guy and give me a chance of escaping after it's over, I'm up for it."

"Come into the study. I'll show you the layout and explain the plan."

PART THREE

MIAMI

18 ••••••

Frank Blackwell arrived at Miami International on an Eastern Airways late-afternoon flight from Newark. Blackwell wore wraparound sunglasses, light-colored slacks, Nike running shoes, and a striped rugby sports shirt. He could have been a tourist, a tout, a T-man, or a terrorist, or even a tungsten salesman. He moved into the airport's twilight world of artificial lighting, canned air, and synthetic music. Unobtrusively he took the escalator down to the lower lobby and claimed his luggage. He went to the Hertz counter and they sent an attendant to get the car he had reserved from Newark International. It was a white Chevrolet Cavalier convertible with automatic shift. Blackwell put his luggage into the trunk and drove out of the concrete and shadow into the air and sunshine of southern Florida.

Miami was moist and steamy, with a sky of blue enamel and cotton clouds glued into place around the horizon. Blackwell took the causeway east to Biscayne, then turned south. At 37th Street he pulled into the parking lot of the Turfrider, a new five-story hotel built of glass and aluminum in the shape of a step pyramid.

The Turfrider had a sweeping driveway lined with bellboys in glittering Michael Jackson–inspired high-collared sequin jackets. Energetic obsequiousness was the order of the day; bowing and scraping as you got

out of your late-model car, flashing smiles and murmured greetings as you glided through the smoked-
glass doors into the cathedrallike expanse of the
main lobby. The interior was done in Mexican Modern. There was a life-size replica of the Aztec calendar stone in bronze set at a tilt on a plinth in the
middle of the lobby. An enormous Dávilos mural of
working-class peasants doing the hat dance occupied
one entire wall. Expensive-looking guests were dot-
ted here and there, star-scattered on the carpeting,
smoking cigars and flashing their teeth. Everyone
moved slowly and rather exquisitely, as though they
were actors in a Broadway musical called *Money with
Taco Sauce.* Stage lighting gave the place a south-of-
the-border Götterdämmerung look.

Blackwell's room had tall french windows and a
balcony with a view of Biscayne Bay. He unpacked
methodically. Took a shower and changed his clothes.
Put on fresh tan slacks, lightweight sports shirt, and
white linen sports jacket. Then telephoned the front
desk. No calls had come in for him. Minska's flight
(they had flown on separate flights for security-related
reasons) was probably late.

Blackwell was getting hungry and he felt like stretching his legs. When he left the hotel, he detected a
movement behind him and to his left. He couldn't be
absolutely sure, but it seemed to him that someone
had stepped out from behind the big potted palm at
the edge of the hotel driveway just as he had reached
the sidewalk.

He walked north on Biscayne to SW 8th Street.
The early-evening sky was a velvet blue. A large and
unreal yellow moon had black palm-tree silhouettes
appliquéd to it. In Miami, even the sky was an advertising gimmick.

Blackwell turned onto SW 8th, the main stem of

Latin Miami. It was impossible to tell if someone was following him or not. He had his suspicions but couldn't be sure. He knew he was going to have to get used to a lot of not being sure. It went with the territory. Uncertainty, that is. There were too many people, too much noise and color, too much high-speed sidewalk action.

A man fell into step beside him. He was a small, skinny man, dark-skinned, with frizzy, tightly curled hair. He had a small silver ring in his left nostril. He wore a yoke-back cowboy shirt and a wide tooled leather belt with silver conchos or whatever the hell they call them set all around. He had on a pair of hand-tooled cowboy boots with toes that tapered to a needle point. He had a red bandanna around his neck held in place by a silver ring set with turquoise. There was no trouble picking him out of a crowd.

Winking at Blackwell, he said, "Hey, baby, you need some action?"

"Fuck off," Blackwell said.

"Hey, come on, man, I'm Eddy López, what they call Fast Eddy, like in the movie, you know?"

Blackwell turned into a restaurant. La Floridita was a long narrow place lit with neon. It had a lunch counter on one side, a row of booths on the other. It was a tamales-and-black-beans sort of place, and there was a stack of *medianoches* near the grill, the toasted ham-and-cheese sandwiches that are the favored late-night snack of many Cubans. Blackwell sat down in a booth in the rear. López followed him and slid onto the bench opposite.

"You like Cuban coffee, man?" López asked. "It's the bes' in the world." He ordered two coffees. "How you like Miami? Anything you want, you speak to me, OK? I don't mean to be obvious, but if you want a woman, or a boy—"

"Oh come on," Blackwell said.

López didn't look abashed. "Lots of businessmen like it. Even if they don't take, they like to be asked."

"I suppose you're also going to offer me dope."

"Sure, man. The best crack in the world."

"Fine. You got anything else?"

"How'd you like to get into a time-sharing condo in Marathon Shores? Full buyout guaranteed in three years."

"Fast Eddy, that sounds more like the real you."

"That's cruel," López said. "We'll talk again soon." He got up abruptly and walked out.

López turned west and went one block, then stopped at a late-model Pontiac double-parked with its motor running. López got into the backseat. The Pontiac drove off. Blackwell watched it go through the neon-streaked glass of the restaurant window. It might have meant something, or it might not have. That was the thing about uncertainty, you were never sure.

When Blackwell returned to the Turfrider there was a message for him at the desk. No name. Just an address.

19 • • • • •

The Hotel Nemo was located in Miami Beach's South Beach section. It was a low lime-green stucco building with a long wooden porch. Old people sat in recliners and lounges on the porch. There were a couple of chickens pecking in the crabgrass, but they probably belonged to the Nueva Buenavista, which adjoined the Nemo. Overhead the huge glowing sun of Miami overflowed with heat and humidity.

The manager wasn't around. But one of the old ladies on the porch, dressed in a soiled muumuu, ravaged face partially concealed by a big straw hat on which was written "Souvenir of the Bahamas," asked Blackwell if she could help.

"Mr. Minska? Signed in yesterday." She had nothing to do but watch people and remember what they looked like in case Metro Squad ever wanted to know. "Big heavy guy without much hair and a big nose, right? Light freckled skin, he should watch out for the sun. Wearing a Hawaiian-type shirt, all reds and greens with black palm trees against a lemon moon. He's got a room on the second floor. Number 23. Such a nice man, quiet-spoken. Are you his brother, maybe?"

"Just a friend," Blackwell said.

"It figures," she said. "You don't really look much like him."

*   *   *

Blackwell went inside, up a flight of creaking steps, down a corridor lit by fifteen-watt lights in the ceiling. The whole inside was peeling, as if it had gotten one sunburn too many. The pastels were the exact shade of hopelessness. The hallway smelled of Campbell's Golden Mushroom Soup.

Blackwell knocked at 23, and Minska let him in. His small room was crammed with a cot and two bureaus, on one of which was a hotplate. In the corner, a miniature refrigerator, just so you could drink yourself into oblivion with chilled wine. Smell of coffee, bourbon, seaweed.

"Good to see you," Minska said.

"What are you doing in a place like this?" Blackwell asked.

"I've got an uncle owns this place. I stay here free."

"Even free is too much."

"Maybe you're right," Minska said. "Come on, we'll go to the Heliogabalus Cafeteria, get their breakfast special."

"It's afternoon, Minska."

"Don't worry, they have the breakfast special all day."

Orange lighting recessed in the ceiling gave a warm glow to the crepuscular skins of the inhabitants, whose average age was about 110. Sandwiches stuffed to sphericity were served by waitresses who were born tired. The owner, whose name was either Max or Harry, sagged in a big armchair near the cash register, balancing in his mind the good sound of money being rung up on the till against the bad sound of the Marielitos breaking crockery in the kitchen. It took them a while before they mastered the dishwashers. Behind the serving counter there were rows of stainless-steel covers beneath which lurked the ubiquitous stuffed cabbage, the brisket of beef, the young tom turkey and his milieu, giblet gravy. There were vats and vats of gravy, because gravy is a good way to get down meat that has been steamed to death.

Blackwell ordered toasted bagel and cream cheese and Minska had the short stack, two over easy, three strips of bacon, hash browns, toast, coffee.

"Look, Minska, let's stop horsing around. We've got work to do. Where the hell were you?"

"What's your rush, kid? We don't get to Miami that often. Don't be in such a hurry."

"I thought we had to move fast. The window of opportunity."

"But we still got time for breakfast and a couple hours on the beach."

"What about the equipment?" Blackwell asked.

"I've got everything upstairs in the room."

"Shouldn't we test it out?"

"No time. We have to get moving on this tonight. Is that fast enough for you?"

"Yes, that's plenty fast enough," Blackwell said. He felt a tightening in his stomach.

20 • • • • •

Soon after midnight they took a taxi to 67th Street and Indian Creek Road. They went into one of Miami Beach's best-known landmarks, Norman's Tavern. It was a quiet, dimly lit saloon with chess tables in the back. The long bar was dark and comfortable, with indirect lighting and Daumier prints on the wall. But what really characterized the place was its music. Many places, and this includes most of Miami, are content to plug into the nearest Muzak outlet and let them serve up the submoron pap used no doubt to pacify crowds with its sweet insistence on "Love ya, baby, yah, yah," and other lyrics of some semiotic interest, perhaps, but not much intellectual content. Cooler places with some aspiration to being with it, places in Coconut Grove desperately trying to flaunt their counterfeit chic, sometimes play approved jazz classics and safe Dixieland. The really trendy bars catering to a young crowd give you heavy metal and Poughkeepsie Violet. Only Norman's had sitar music and Turkish progressive jazz played by the Istanbul Five.

Into Norman's Tavern came some of the shadiest characters in South Florida, the Key Largo rednecks as well as the Baker's Haulover white-collar smugglers. Norman's was that sort of a place. It didn't matter what you did or were planning to do. The rule was, don't do it in Norman's. If there was an altercation, Norman's main bartender, Big Kate, was usually able to handle it. Norman himself, slouching in a corner of the bar, a bohemian figure in his black turtleneck sweater and stretch Levi's, took it all in and kept it all to himself.

Norman bade Minska a courteous hello, nodded to Blackwell, welcomed them to his saloon, and set them up two beers on the house.

"That guy knows us now," Blackwell said.

"Norman knows everything happens in this town," Minska said. "But he never tells. Where did you put your bag?"

Each man had entered the bar with a long nylon zip bag.

"It's here under my feet."

"OK. Now listen, here's how we're going to do this."

Blackwell had a lot of faith in Minska. But later, when they had silently eased themselves into the dark, oily waters of the Intracoastal Waterway just three blocks from Norman's Tavern, adjusted their respirators and face masks, and slid underwater for the three-quarter-mile swim to the big drainpipe that lay just below the surface of Framijian's seawall on the other side of Indian Creek, he wasn't so sure.

21 • • • • •

Blackwell swam with an economical sidestroke, dragging behind him the waterproof bag which contained his weapons, clothing, cigarettes, loose change, and Swiss army knife. The water was brackish and tasted of old coffee grounds. A muted hum of traffic like giant vibrating insects came from the nearby 79th Street Causeway.

Blackwell was a good swimmer. He stayed just behind and to the right of Minska, who also moved through the water with an economical sidestroke, his hooded head just below the surface. Blackwell smelled orange peel, the state aroma, and dead seagull. The sweet-sour odor of water hyacinth mingled with gasoline fumes was a perfume so ubiquitous as to seem something nature herself had dreamed up.

The waterway was no more than half a mile wide at this point. Blackwell tried to make out landmarks, but with his head at water level it was difficult. Little lights winked from the homes along the shore. A boat passed within twenty yards of him, a white sport fisherman trailing seagulls and a sound of rock music. He submerged until it passed.

The water was warm, and the air temperature was in the eighties. Blackwell felt the intoxication that comes from engaging in a dangerous action without too much reflection.

They submerged again when an open launch filled

with hilarious teenagers roared past them. Then they took up the stroke again. Soon they were across the waterway, swimming parallel to the bulkheaded artificial islands on the Miami side. Blackwell marveled at what a great sense of direction Minska must have, for they were just inside the loops of canals that made up Normandy Isles. From water level, everything looked the same—just a whole lot of canals with houses set back from the bulkheads and surrounded by dense shrubbery.

Then Minska stopped and gestured to Blackwell to swim closer.

"What's up?" Blackwell asked.

"It all looks the same," Minska said.

"You mean you're lost?"

"No, I'm not lost. Just a little disoriented. They really ought to have signs you can read from the water."

"You mean you don't know where we are?"

"Of course I know, but not exactly."

"So what do we do now?"

"I think we'd better go ashore and find out."

It was quiet on the little islets connected by roads and bridges that made up Normandy Isles. The streets were empty. A streetlight here and there glowed through the surrounding trees. Normandy Isles was at this point like a small river delta with canals radiating from it in various directions like spokes from a central hub. In the dark, illuminated only by the tricky flat lighting of a cloud-tossed moon, the various canals were indistinguishable from one another.

Minska found a gap between two properties where the shore sloped high enough so they could scramble ashore. They were standing at the end of a dead-end street. Cars were parked here and there. Flickering colored lights through big picture windows revealed late-night TV.

They slung their fins and face masks into their waterproof sacks and began to walk, searching for a road sign, or any other sort of a sign. The street curved and wavered and twisted and turned, streetlights seemed to be going out of style, and street signs were nonexistent.

Then they saw the man walking up the street toward them. He was a short little guy wearing shorts and a short-sleeved white shirt that glowed in the dark. He was walking an animal, some sort of a little mutt dog. The man hesitated as he caught a look at Blackwell and Minska. With their black rubber swimming gear and waterproof rubber bags slung over their shoulders and their swim masks perched on their foreheads, they looked like advance scouts for an invasion of the Fish People. Once the short little guy got a good look at them he plainly would have preferred to be somewhere else, like in a bar in Nacogdoches, Texas, maybe, but it was too late, the two black-rubber crazies were walking up to him and one of them was saying, "Excuse me, sir, what is the name of this street?"

Now he'd heard everything—a couple of guys dressed in black rubber from head to toe and dripping wet asking the name of his street. After this they'd kill him, of course, and it was his own fault, he should never have left the house without his good ole army .45.

"This is Sea Grape Lane," he said, expecting the worst.

His dog, sensing trouble, was crouching behind his leg, whimpering.

"Aha," said the questioner. "*Sea Grape*, of course!

In that case Flamingo Drive must be two streets over to the left."

"That's right," the little guy told him. "It's the block past Dolphin Shores."

"I shoulda known it," the questioner said. "Thanks, mister." The two guys in the frog suits walked off in the direction they'd come from—the dead-end street. As for the short, shorts-clad dog walker, he turned around and went back the way he'd come too, back home, fast, his dog leading the way and tugging at the leash. I mean, look at it this way—when dripping wet black rubber crazies are walking around asking street directions, it's time to get under cover and double-lock the doors and load the .45 and let the dog piss on the rug if he really has to go.

Back in the water, Minska led them unerringly around a bend, into a canal, and then into a sharp right around another canal. "Here it is," he told Blackwell.

Blackwell, treading water, saw a property that came down to the water's edge. It was protected by a ten-foot-high chain-link fence topped with barbed wire and rigged with sensors. A sign in the middle of it said, "This property protected by the Midas Thunderbolt Protection Corporation. Caution, plenty high voltage." Behind the fence, lit by the baleful white eye of the malevolent moon, a large house hunkered down behind dense shrubbery like an apocalyptic stucco beast grazing on landfill.

"OK," Minska said. "Now to find that drainpipe." Adjusting his face mask, he dove below the surface. After a few moments he came up again. "I need you to hold the flashlight," he said to Blackwell.

He and Blackwell went down again. By the strong white beam of the waterproof flashlight Blackwell could see a large round grille set into the bulkhead about five feet below the surface. While he held the flashlight, Minska opened a small pack strapped to his waist and removed a screwdriver. He worked with it for a moment, then rose to the surface, gesturing Blackwell to follow him.

"What's the matter?" Blackwell asked.

"I need a Phillips."

"I thought you had all the tools we needed."

"How was I supposed to know they fastened this thing with Phillips-head screws?"

"I think I have one on my Swiss army knife," Blackwell said. "But it's in my little tool kit, inside my waterproof bag."

"So? Let me have it."

With Minska's help, Blackwell tugged open a zipper. Warm, garbage-scented water flooded his waterproof bag, which lived up to its description by not letting a drop of it out once it was zipped again. He managed to get his knife and handed it to Minska. In a few minutes Minska had the grating open.

After that, it was simple enough to squirm up through the curving tube with its three-foot diameter to the dry concrete catchment tank that lay a meter within Framijian's property. Arming themselves, they went on to the house, which lay before them silent and dark like a sphinx of cariocas.

22 •••••

Ever since his American-born wife, Rosalie, had left him, taking with her their two-year-old daughter, Hannah, Framijian lived alone in his house on Venetian Isle. He had almost an acre of land and a hundred feet of frontage. His house was protected by a barbed-wire fence equipped with state-of-the-art sensors. The fence itself was concealed behind high green hedges. Near the house, with its sweeping drive, was an Olympic-size swimming pool. Bits and pieces of statuary were scattered around the landscaped grounds.

He was a careful man, but not unduly security-conscious. He had never had any trouble with anyone. No one hassled a gun dealer unless he was angry at him, and Framijian was friends with everyone.

His living room was bright with mobiles and cubistic paintings. There were books on the wall, all the best titles, in uniform editions, with a place of honor for the Harvard Classics and the Hundred Greatest Books. Morning sunlight winked off the cut-glass decanters on the sideboard loaded with rare single-malt whiskies. His wine closet was just off the kitchen. He had a collection of vintages which might have stocked a small restaurant.

Framijian himself, a slim small man with a round skull topped by close-cropped curly black hair just beginning to be touched with gray, entered his own living room. He was whistling to himself. It was ten-thirty in the morning, his usual hour of rising. He was dressed in a blue silk dressing robe. There were black leather huaraches on his feet. He wore an antique Roman gold coin around his neck on a finely woven gold chain; all the dope dealers were wearing them this season and Framijian liked to stay in fashion.

There was something that seemed strange about the living room this morning. But he couldn't figure out what it was. Everything looked as it ought to look, yet something was different. He compared the present room with a pattern he held in his mind, a pattern showing all the room's objects and their relationships to each other and to the walls, floor, and ceiling, showing even the way the sun, slanting in through the jalousies, lighted everything differently depending on the time of day.

That was it. Something was different about the lighting.

Then he noticed that the venetian blind had been raised, not much, just an inch or so, but enough to allow a beam of light to penetrate to a part of the room it usually didn't get to.

His mind was working furiously. He had to assume that someone was in the room. And he had to assume that whoever it was meant him no good.

The transition from complete peace to all-out crisis was shockingly quick. Beads of sweat broke out on his forehead. No more than a second had elapsed since he had noticed the raised blind, and he knew it was time he did something, because it was important that he not betray his knowledge of the intruder. He forced himself to take another step into the room, a room that had changed suddenly from a refuge into a trap. In an instant he had his moves planned out.

He turned, as if he had forgotten something, tapping his head lightly with the forefinger of his right hand, and smiling, silly me, I forgot the ... He started back through the doorway, toward the .357 Magnum he kept in a clip under the oiled walnut table in the hall.

But suddenly there was a man standing in front of him, a big man wearing a black wetsuit and carrying a gun. Where the hell had he come from? And then there was another man, also in a wetsuit. The intruders' feet made no sound on the deep pile of his carpet. Framijian cringed as one of them, the big, burly one, leveled his piece at Framijian's head.

Framijian's mouth opened but no words came out. He dropped to his knees. The man rested the muzzle of the gun against Framijian's forehead. Framijian could see his finger tighten around the trigger, see the hammer on the big blue steel automatic begin to lift. Tears came to Framijian's eyes, his bones turned to water, he cringed, eyes fixed on the foreshortened automatic.

"For God's sake," he said, "at least wait until I say the *sh'ma.*"

The trigger snapped.

The hammer fell on an empty chamber.

Framijian felt as if someone had pulled the plugs out from behind his knees. He fell to the floor.

Somebody was shaking him. "Don't faint," the big, older guy told him. "Keep on tracking if you want to stay alive."

"All right," Framijian said, fighting the urge to sink into the safety of unconsciousness.

The man said to him, very seriously, "That was the rehearsal." He jacked a round into the chamber of his automatic. "Next time it's a take. Got it?"

"Yes," Framijian said, his heart hammering so hard it seemed to be coming through his chest.

"You *can* come out of this alive, Framijian," the big man said, "but you have to be very careful, do exactly what you're told, and not try to put one over on us. Understood?"

Framijian shuddered, wiped his face, fought to get control of himself. He was still shaking, but his well-honed sense of survival was taking over. He didn't speak until he could trust his voice not to break.

"Let me get up," Framijian said. He got up off the floor shakily and sat down in one of the big armchairs. "Anybody got a cigarette? I think there's a pack on my desk."

The older man gave him the pack and a lighter. Framijian lit up. He could remember the *sh'ma* now, but maybe it wouldn't be necessary.

"Look," Framijian said, "I'm a realist. You've got me, OK? Tell me what you want me to do and I'll do it."

Neither man answered him. Framijian went on, "If you'd come here to kill me, I'd be dead by now. So you want something else. Whatever it is, I'll give it to you. I figure if I play this very cool I can come out alive. I mean, I think there's a good chance you won't kill me if I cooperate. I know, it's a calculated risk, but what the hell, it's the only play I've got. Okay so far?"

"Sounds good," the big man said.

"This isn't anything simple, like robbery, is it?"

"Right," the younger man said.

"But there's something you want me to do?"

"Right again."

"So how can I help you?" Framijian said. "What do you want me to do?"

The big man said, "My friend here has to meet Alfonso Guzmán."

Framijian needed a moment to take it in. Then he realized that these men knew about the arms deal. And there could be only one reason why they wanted to meet Guzmán.

"I can arrange that," Framijian said. He was starting to feel better. Thank God, there was always an angle. "Can we go into the kitchen, make some coffee, discuss this?"

Half an hour later, over cups of steaming espresso, Framijian was saying, "OK, you want to knock off Guzmán. Here's what we do. You'll go to him as my representative. You and he will agree on a time and place for him to take the arms and give you the money. How does that sound?"

"Not bad," the big man said. "Not bad at all."

"Then let's go over the whole thing step by step. Would you mind if I put up another pot of coffee? We have some planning to do."

Framijian was adaptable.

23 • • • • •

Guzmán telephoned promptly at nine that evening.

"How is everything?" Guzmán asked.

"Fine, fine," Framijian said. "Couldn't be better." The nose of the big man's automatic was pointed directly at his left eye. A ray of lamplight lit the barrel of the gun, at the rear of which sat the bullet. Framijian could see only a little way into the barrel. It looked blue-black and slick: passageway to hell. The other guy, younger, skinnier, was sitting on the couch reading Volume 1 of *The Discourses of Epictetus* in the Loeb edition.

"We need to meet," Guzmán said. "Set up the final details."

"Yes," Framijian said. "Just what I was thinking. I'm going to send someone over."

"You are?" Guzmán was suspicious of any change in routine. "Why not come yourself??"

Framijian had been hastily trying to invent a reason in the brief time he'd had before the call. It wasn't fair, them not giving him enough time to prepare a good enough cover story to save his life.

Well, he'd thought of something, and it just would have to do.

"I'm laid up for a few days," Framijian said. "You ever hear of the gout?"

"What's that?" Guzmán asked.

"It's a disease of the big toe." If they'd given him time, he could have looked up the Spanish for gout. Not that an ex-commander of the model prison in Managua should be expected to know the Spanish word for gout. Probably didn't come across it much in his line of work.

"Yeah, I heard of that." Guzmán was indeed a man of unexpected resources.

"It comes and it goes. Hereditary. Right now it's got me laid up. I just have to sit in bed for a while with my foot on a pillow until the medicine takes hold. Three days, a week at the most."

"Sorry to hear it," Guzmán said.

"But of course I'm here to talk to you on the phone anytime. And I'm going to send my sister's husband, Frank, absolutely trustworthy, you'll like him."

"Where's he from, this Frank?" Guzmán said. "You never mentioned him before."

"Well, of course not, he's an American, but he's married to my sister Leah and they were in Haifa, looking after the family shipping interests."

"Does he speak English?"

"Of course," Framijian said. "I told you, he's an American."

"You're sure he's OK?"

"I'd trust him with my life," Framijian said. "I've brought him back to America because I need his help."

"OK," Guzmán said. "Send him tomorrow for lunch."

Guzmán hung up. Framijian also hung up, taking care not to clink the handcuffs that secured him by a length of chain to a hot-water pipe. He looked at Minska.

Minska hung up the extension phone. "You did

good," he said. "You just keep on like that, you're going to come out of this all right."

"I told you I was cooperative," Framijian said. "How about taking off the cuffs?"

"We'll leave them on to spare you temptation."

"Well then, how about some dinner?" Framijian said. "I mean, they feed hostages, don't they? And how am I supposed to go to the bathroom, you know, number two?"

"We'll discuss those matters in a few minutes," Minska said. "Just now I need to talk about a couple of things with my partner. You won't mind if we use the dining room?"

"Be my guest," Framijian said, with an abbreviated wave of his cuffed hands.

"OK," Minska said to Blackwell, "you're set up for lunch tomorrow with your Victim. You know how to get there, right?"

"I've rented a car," Blackwell said.

"OK. Now, think about this, Frank. I know it may seem a little early in the acquaintanceship, but it wouldn't be a bad idea if you killed Guzmán tomorrow and got it over with. After coffee, perhaps. And after you get a check for the weapons. When you get the check, put it into this envelope and mail it first chance you get."

The envelope was addressed to a box number in Morristown, New Jersey. Blackwell put it into his pocket.

"I was meaning to ask you," Blackwell said. "Just how, exactly, should I go about killing him? I mean, I'm going to be in the middle of his property and it might look a little suspicious if I pulled out a handgun and blew him away."

Minska looked offended. "I'm your Spotter! I'd

never let you use a gun in a situation like that. I don't even want you carrying one. I think one of the new techniques is called for. Did they tell you about the Killer Roadmap Trick?"

"I never did finish New Techniques class," Blackwell said.

"Doesn't matter, it's perfectly simple. Just lucky I happen to have a prototype killer roadmap with me." He rummaged in his waterproof bag and came up with a flat envelope wrapped in oiled paper. Drawing on gloves, he opened the envelope and unfolded the map within.

"Don't touch it yet. Looks like a standard Exxon roadmap, of Dade County, right? Wrong. One of the edges of this roadmap is razor-sharp. The idea is to hand it to your Victim, assuming that he's still unsuspecting, of course, and ask him where to find somewhere or other. Let's say you ask him where's the Seaquarium. When he takes the map in his hand you give a very slight pull, accidental-like, and the edge slips through his fingers and gives him a paper cut. People get them every day—nothing to worry about."

"But this is to worry about, right?"

"You better believe it. That edge is coated with Cossacks Three, a new Soviet poison extracted from louse dung. The poison mimics the onset of flu complicated by hypochondria. Onset is in a few hours, so you should be able to get away without difficulty. What's the matter?"

"I was just thinking," Blackwell said. "It's sort of rude to kill a man on the first day you meet him after eating his lunch."

"Don't worry about manners," Minska growled. "This is the Hunt."

"I know. I was just being silly," Blackwell said.

"What we'll do, you'll go out the front door very

quietly and walk down to the 79th Street Causeway and get a taxi. It's pitch-black out there; no one's going to see a thing. Get yourself a good night's sleep. It's going to be a big day tomorrow. Remember to kill Guzmán only *after* you get the check. The Hunt needs all the financing it can get. Immediately after the kill, phone me here. We'll decide the next move then."

While they conferred, Framijian had had a chance to find an old Fifth Avenue candy bar in the upper-left-hand drawer of his desk. He munched and chuckled to himself. These hijackers thought they were so smart, but there was one thing they didn't know about despite all their advance briefing. They didn't know that behind a panel with a trick opening in the rumpus room there was a small, powerful radio transmitter. They didn't know that Framijian was supposed to make a transmission every night at midnight.

And since they didn't know that, they also didn't know that when he failed to make his transmission, some heavy people on Outer Cay were going to get extremely upset.

And then it was going to get interesting.

24 •••••

The radio mast was the highest structure on Outer Cay. In combination with the motor-driven dish antennas mounted on the roof of the main building, it could pull in signals from all over the world. Its main function was to receive the nightly calls from Bahamas Corporation operatives all over the Western Hemisphere. These signals were usually sent in concentrated two-second bursts, and were unintelligible to anyone without sophisticated recording and unscrambling equipment. The call showed that the operative was in place and business was going on as usual. To fail to report was serious. If you didn't broadcast at your appointed time, you were expected to come on the air two hours later, and to provide a good explanation at the annual regional meeting of your branch of the organization.

When Framijian failed to report by five past eleven local time, the chief radio operator informed Director Dahl. Dahl waited another hour, then, following the corporation's regulations, telephoned the company whose job it was to look into irregularities.

The operative's name was Mercedes Brannigan. At this time she was closing a case in Victoria, capital of the independent kingdom of Salambak.

25 • • • • •

We are looking into a tropical dining room, all bamboo and rattan. There are big fans overhead. They turn slowly, pushing around the moist, sluggish air. Throughout the restaurant there are spectacular displays of tropical plants: entire banana trees, fig trees, growing out of huge tubs carved from the local lava. Waiters pass slowly back and forth among the diners. From the red-and-black-striped turbans on their heads, the experienced traveler can tell that these are Bajau, one of the indigenous peoples of this part of Borneo.

Not so many years ago, they were headhunters and cannibals. There has even been some rumor that they continue these activities to the present day. Not that the government of Salambak, the tiny independent kingdom so recently sprung into being, permits that sort of thing.

The diners are few, and mostly elderly. This is the oldest restaurant on this part of the coast, the finest restaurant in all Borneo. Not many can afford to eat here.

The diners are the few remaining survivors of the old aristocracy, which was annihilated in the violence that accompanied the overthrow of the government some two months ago and the installation of the new government under Heeter Dyal, the newly proclaimed

President for Eternity of the North Borneo Republic of Salambak.

The President for Eternity enters now. He wears the golden arm rings of royalty set with the huge rubies of the Altenback Mine in the interior of the republic. Salambak is a prosperous little country. There are rubies, ebony and other rare woods in its jungles, rare spices from its alluvial valleys.

The former government was conservative. There was still money in the royal treasury when Dyal and his ragtag army of tribal brothers looted it. The revolution boiled up so swiftly and unexpectedly that the old prime minister didn't have time to make the final transfers to his Swiss bank account. He died in a hail of bullets amid a welter of checkbooks, his helicopter still warming up on the well-trimmed lawn outside the Presidential Palace.

In view of the country's general prosperity, you would have thought Salambak could pay off at least its most urgent debts. But such was not the case. The country was broke, or so the new President for Eternity maintained to his creditors. One of these creditors, the Bahamas Corporation, had demanded an explanation, and had finally sent its representative, Miss Mercedes Brannigan, to ascertain the reasons for herself.

Mercedes had just arrived. She was a stunning woman, her hair the blue-black that you see from time to time among the Celts, her skin the palest olive, a memento of the Castilian ancestry on her mother's side. She floated into the room dressed in a finely cut white linen suit.

Heeter Dyal rose and greeted her. He was not himself a pure Dyak. The Andaman Islands was in his blood, and a touch of the Pathan as well, inherited from an adventurous great-grandmother who had been a victualer for the British at the time of the Second Afghan War.

Heeter Dyal was suave, affable. "My dear Miss Brannigan, Mercedes, if I may, how delighted I am to be able to greet you on behalf of my government and myself. We were delighted when our foreign office received your telegram advising us of your visit. You had no difficulties at customs, I assume?"

"None whatsoever," Mercedes said. "Your people didn't even look at my luggage."

"But of course not! I thought that that was understood. I told your people that Rolexes sell very well here on the black market. You can tell all of your friends that too. Any friend of the Bahamas Corporation is a friend of mine."

"That's good of you," Mercedes said, not failing to conceal the amusement in her voice at this petty attempt at bribery.

"You can, of course, bring in any amount of currency you want, and an unlimited supply of drugs, whether for your own personal use or for resale. You'll find our minor children a very good market. There are too many of them anyway, so you would be doing all of us a favor if your substances were to kill off a few accidentally. I hope that doesn't sound too callous, but there's only so much of the good stuff to go around."

"Your Excellency," Mercedes said, a little exasperated, "I haven't come here to trade in Rolexes or smuggle drugs. The Bahamas Corporation doesn't go in for that sort of thing."

"I didn't mean to imply that it did," Dyal said, "but I know that you do finance revolutions. After all, I came to power only with your help . . . for which I'll be eternally grateful, by the way. I merely thought that if you or your people wanted to make a little profit on the side—"

"What we would like, Your Excellency," Mercedes said, "is to be repaid the money we advanced so you could arm your men, bug the Presidential Palace, and suborn the army."

"But of course," Dyal said. "Please submit your bill at your earliest possible convenience."

"We have already sent it, Your Excellency," Mercedes said.

"You have?"

"Several times, by registered letter, which Your Excellency was good enough to sign for. I have the receipts here in my handbag."

"Then there must have been some mistake," Dyal said with an easy smile. "You know I'm good for it."

"There's no doubt of that," Mercedes said, "but the Bahamas Corporation has a policy. After the third request for payment goes unanswered, they send me."

"And what do you do, my dear?"

"I close the account."

Dyal smiled faintly, which gave to his flat, small-featured face a look of sinister malevolence accentuated by his underdeveloped earlobes. He looked swiftly around. His superb peripheral vision enabled him to take in his bodyguard of sharpshooters in the restaurant's upper gallery, their guns trained on the woman.

"I hope you are not thinking of offering me violence in my own country," Dyal said. "My bodyguard has been trained to respond quickly to any gesture I may make. If you tried to assassinate me, you'd never get out the door."

"Don't be silly," Mercedes said. "You'll settle up this time, won't you?"

"Of course, as soon as we can get the accounts together. Our check will be in the mail at the end of the week at the latest."

"I see. So there's no problem. And now, can we order some of your chef's special cuisine, which is at least half the reason I made the trip here in the first place?"

"You've heard about our chef!" Dyal said, beaming.

"Of course. I read the write-up on him in *Great Chefs of Asia Quarterly.* I have been longing ever since to sample his dibbelbikker dishes."

"So you know about that, too," Dyal said, delighted. "Yes. Our famous old cannibal cuisine. Nowadays, we do not eat humans, but there are many remarkable and tasty dishes from the old days that we can prepare using special spices to simulate the real thing. Surgium powder, for example, is an almost perfect culinary substitute for Caucasian fingernail shavings, and in order to prepare sweet metatarsal stew ... well, all the real metatarsals have died out now, you know. They were small pig-like beasts about the size of a quirrumburry. Never mind, we find substitutes. Comparative phylogeny is a fine thing, is it not?"

"It is very interesting," Mercedes said. "Your cook must be a genius. All the food magazines say so."

"Oh, he is first-rate, of course. He's the only man left in the world who still knows how to cook in the dibbelbikker style. Most of our people, despite their backgrounds, have never tasted those dishes."

"Why is that?"

"Because cannibalism has been forbidden and substitute meat is very expensive. Ah, but here comes the chef."

A short plump man, dressed all in white, with a white chef's cap, came up to their table.

"Excellency. So delighted to see you this afternoon."

The two men performed the intricate hand gestures ending with the one that signifies "This is a duck," and nodded to each other in a friendly way.

"Is the feast ready, then?" Dyal asked.

"There is a difficulty," the chef confessed.

"What is it?"

"Sire, I will have to show you."

The chef led the mystified President for Eternity into the kitchen. Mercedes sat alone at the table. She kept her back very straight. It was how she had been taught as a child. She looked up to the gallery and saw the bodyguard watching her from behind pointed rifles.

Mercedes called out to them, in grammatical Dyak, although with a slight Zamboangan accent. "Point those guns elsewhere, please."

There were six bodyguards packed tightly together in the narrow second-floor gallery. Their rifles were old bolt-action Springfields. They wore tan uniforms with khaki belts. They all looked rather alike, as members of the same bodyguard tend to do after a while. One of them was taller than the others, and his polished gray sharkskin badge of rank marked him as a man a cut above the others.

He said, "Where Boss?" His voice was low, flat, uninflected, but the slight tension that tightened his hand on the Springfield under his arm did not pass unnoticed by the attractive dark-haired girl who sat twenty feet in front and below him on the suddenly empty floor of the only three-star restaurant in all of North Borneo.

"Boss be right back," Mercedes said. "He gone men's room."

The bodyguard's face quirked into a rictus of indecision as circuits of his mind, long deadened by years of smoking quat and chewing ergant, wrestled with the problem of where all this fit into the scheme of things. The Boss's absence could be entirely innocent . . . if peeing could ever be considered innocent. On the other hand, the Boss usually held up one finger when he went to the john. It was perplexing.

And then from the kitchen stepped the chef, holding aloft a steaming platter from beneath whose silver cover effused tangy and unusual meaty fragrances with more than a hint of lemon and ginger sauce.

"My friends," the chef said, addressing the six bodyguards, "thanks to the miracle of modern microwave and pressure cooking techniques, I am pleased to invite the six of you to be the first Dyaks of your generation to partake of the legendary dibbelbikker cuisine of our ancestors in all its authenticity."

He indicated a table set with service for six. "Please come down from the gallery and enjoy the feast. And then shake hands with our new President for Eternity, my brother, Ernon."

Ernon came out from the kitchen, tall and balding, smiling and waving. The bodyguards were intelligent enough to perceive that there had been a change of fortune. They could, of course, kill everyone present in retaliation, and that thought did occur to them; but they were quick to perceive the practical advantages of starting out on the right foot with the new regime. And, of course, they had always wanted to try the genuine dibbelbikker cannibal cuisine. They cheered once, their voices restrained but respectful, then came down to the main restaurant floor.

The chef's brother, Ernon, clasped Mercedes gratefully by the hand.

"We owe it all to you, Miss Brannigan. You have helped us to rid ourselves of the tyrant, Dyal."

"I had to do it," Mercedes replied. "The company rule is very strict. All loans must be repaid when promised. We don't care where you get it from, but you must get it. That's the only reliable basis on which foreign and illegal businesses can operate, but Dyal forgot that."

"He thought he was safe within his own restaurant," Ernon mused. "Within the heart of his own country."

"Let it be a warning to everyone," Mercedes said. "I mean, I don't want to belabor the obvious, but I must point out again that the corporation doesn't like to be toyed with."

"I have already paid you, of course," Ernon said hastily. "You do remember? I gave you the check in my office."

"Of course," Mercedes said. "Don't worry."

"Perhaps you would like a little more?" Ernon asked, taking out his checkbook. "For your trouble, I mean."

"No trouble," Mercedes said. "And no thank you. I don't accept any unauthorized money. I am a representative of the Bahamas Corporation, and we only want what is owed us."

"Praise Allah you are reasonable people," Ernon said. "Would you care to join us in the feast?"

Mercedes shook her head. "No thank you. I've had all of Dyal I can stomach."

Ernon bowed. Just then a bellboy came running into the dining room from the adjacent hotel.

"Missy Blannigan! Telegram for you!"

Mercedes took it, opened it, and read: "Report Sector Two Tango Charlie soonest."

Mercedes wasted no time packing. This particular job was finished. Her position as an enforcer for the Bahamas Corporation had carried her to many strange places in her two years with the firm. Now she was going to the Bahamas. But she wasn't excited. That was the bad thing about killing people on a regular basis. It rendered you blasé to so much else.

26 ••••••

The seaplane flew in from the southeast, its motor humming in the vast empty sky of the Bahamas like a gigantic mosquito.

"That's Outer Cay right down there," the pilot told her. His name was Jeffrey Blair and he was a private charterer who worked out of Saukie Field, one of Nassau's private commercial airstrips. Mercedes had engaged him to take her to the island.

Mercedes looked down through the cracked plastic. She saw a small shrimp-shaped island set in a wrinkled blue ocean beneath a smoldering midafternoon Caribbean sun.

"It's five point seven miles long by two miles wide," Blair told her. "The harbor is man-made, dredged to a mean depth of ten feet at the gas dock."

Blair circled above the tangled mangroves at the southern end of the island. As they came around the northern end, Mercedes saw the corporation's large, rambling house set in a grove of coconut palms. Nearby were low whitewashed bungalows, and beyond them various sheds and outbuildings.

"Hope you got your invitation handy," Blair said. "They don't take kindly to strangers down there. Privately owned, you know."

"I know," Mercedes said.

"It's a funny sort of place," Blair continued. "Supposed to be staffed by scientists from all over the world. Sort of a think-tank place, isn't it?"

"Sort of," Mercedes said.

"And that's the sort of work you do, too?"

"Something like that," Mercedes said.

"Imagine just sitting around thinking all day," Blair said, in tones that revealed that he for one couldn't. "Nice life for some people. Far from worldly cares and all that sort of thing, eh?"

"Ivory tower," Mercedes agreed.

Blair landed and taxied up to the pier. Chardar, a Nepalese micropaleologist from the company's Himalayan center, was there to greet Mercedes. He took her luggage and brought her to the main house. From the veranda they watched Blair take off, his little float plane dwindling swiftly into the cirrus-streaked immensities of the Bahamian sky.

Mercedes said, "Let me show you my credentials."

"That will be all right, Miss Brannigan," Chardar said. "You were expected. Perhaps Dr. Dahl will want to look at them."

"Where is Dr. Dahl?"

"He's chairing a meeting of the Projects Committee. Shall I take you to him?"

"No, I don't want to interrupt. Perhaps I could wait in Dr. Dahl's suite until he's finished?"

"Right this way, miss," Chardar said.

The main building of the Bahamas Corporation was a large, low-slung mansion, part of it executive offices, the rest made up of apartments with terrace and ocean view. There were also chalets with their own beach frontage. Dahl had a five-room apartment. Inside, Mercedes discarded the severely tailored business suit she had worn on the jetliner. She changed into a skimpy two-piece bathing suit which set off her finely proportioned figure to advantage. A gossamer white peignoir provided a soft focus for her body. The Olympic-size swimming pool just beyond Dahl's veranda looked inviting. She slid open the glass doors and went out to it at once. Mercedes never lost a chance for a swim between kills.

The role of enforcer, button man, field executive, or whatever you want to call it has historically been an important one in illegal organizations.

At first, the Bahamas Corporation subcontracted that sort of rough work to various criminal organizations. But the results had not been good. Criminals were ideologically disreputable, and in an organization as idealistic as the Bahamas Corporation, that made a difference.

Nor was it necessary to use them. A Bahamas Corporation secret study showed that some highly respected members of the scientific community were well suited to the perpetration of desperate deeds, as long as those deeds were in a good cause. This was the case with Mercedes.

British-born, she had received her undergraduate education at the University of Cambridge and her graduate training at the University of Oxford. She had held various research and fellowship grants in Canada and the United States in support of her work on visual processing. She was an active and athletic young woman, with well-honed skills at small-arms firing and car racing. Her file had been studied carefully by the Secret Scientific Central. It was decided that an approach would be made when an opportunity presented itself.

The opportunity came that summer. Mercedes went to Italy for a semester of study with the Club of Rome. It was there that she met Arthur Selkirk, the Nobel Prize winner in astrophysics and one of the executives of the Secret Scientific Central. The meeting seemed accidental, though Selkirk had set it up with some care. In the course of their conversation Selkirk noted that the young girl was fearless and well coordinated, honest and well-groomed, self-possessed and ambitious.

At their next meeting, Selkirk described the goals of the Bahamas Corporation, explained what her work would be, and offered her a starting salary of sixty-two thousand dollars a year.

"That's only a beginning, of course," he said. "An entry-level salary. I'm embarrassed at having to offer you so little, but one of the corporation bylaws requires us to keep all entrants at that salary for a year, to see how they work out."

"And if they do work out?" Mercedes asked.

"Then, to use a colloquialism, the sky's the limit. It's not so easy to find people of executive level who can kill, quietly and without a fuss, when the situation calls for it, and who also have good grooming and speak respectable English."

"I want to help save the earth," Mercedes said. "Where do I sign?"

That had been almost three years ago. She had trained for her work, first in Geneva, then in the London branch office in Knightsbridge. Her first field assignments were as understudy to Kristal Karter, the most successful assassin of the decade, sharing a two-bedroom apartment with her in the rue des Halles in Paris, accompanying her on two assignments, but never getting to pull the trigger herself. Kristal had the matador attitude; she always did her own kills.

Now Kristal was dead, the bizarre victim of a traffic accident in Barcelona while returning from a massacre in Málaga. And now Mercedes was a full-fledged enforcer, with a kill in Borneo added to the many to her credit and another in Miami coming up.

It was a considerable responsibility for a twenty-four-year-old girl.

Dahl joined her beside the pool and explained the situation. The Bahamas Corporation needed to find out what had happened to their arms dealer associate Yitzhak Framijian, and why it had happened. And then stop it from ever happening again.

Mercedes was briefed on Alfonso Guzmán and was given the names of people she could call on in Miami for assistance and backup. Dahl suggested that she take the morning mail plane to Nassau and then the regular flight to Miami. But Mercedes had a different idea.

"I'll take that little speedboat you've got anchored off the main dock."

"Is that wise? The Gulf Stream can kick up suddenly at this time of year."

"Don't worry. I'm a good sailor."

Two hours later, Dahl waved goodbye to her as she let loose the mooring lines and set a course for the outer breakwater light. With a fair wind, she expected to be in Miami by late morning.

27 •••••

The small, fast speedboat moved at an easy speed across a moderate chop. Orion rose, the waves blew back foam and the good smell of salt, and the moon peeked in and out of small clouds.

Mercedes adjusted her course to allow for the northward set of the Gulf Stream. It was good to be out alone on the water. Just before dawn she made out low lights on the Florida coast. Soon she could see that she was almost level with Baker's Haulover above Miami. She had missed Government Cut by ten miles or so. She altered course and ran south parallel with the Florida coastline. She was at Government Cut by noon, but it looked too crowded with freighters coming and going from Dodge Island. She continued south and entered Biscayne Bay through Bear Cut, around the southern end of Virginia Key, then crossed the bay and tied up at the gas dock of Forbes' Shipyard in Silver Bluff, just north of the big Dinner Key Marina.

She went to the dockmaster's office and arranged for a place to leave the boat. She rented a car from an Avis agency on the pier and drove to the little house that the Bahamas Corporation maintained in Coconut Grove. She opened it up, turned on the air conditioning, took a shower, and changed into a cool backless dress. Then she telephoned Framijian.

A voice said, "Framijian. Who's this?"

Mercedes pursed her lips and quietly hung up the telephone. She made herself a mild gin and tonic.

Framijian hadn't made his required radio transmission. Nor had he made any attempt in the last twenty-four hours to get in touch with the Bahamas Corporation. Yet here he was in his house answering his telephone.

Conclusion: assuming that the guy who answered the phone *was* Framijian, somebody had to be holding a gun on him. Somebody who didn't know about the radio transmission.

That was exactly the situation the radio-transmission setup was supposed to reveal. Now it was her job to find out exactly what was going on, and who was making it go on. And then to do something about it.

She looked through the little list of southern Florida telephone numbers that Dahl had given her. She called Antonio Alvarez, introduced herself, and explained briefly what she wanted him to do.

28 • • • • •

Antonio Alvarez lived in a luxury penthouse on Brickell near Alice Wainwright Park. But he did his business at the Tropicabana Nightclub on SW 17th.

He drove up in his white 912 Porsche, turned it over to a fawning attendant, threw his cashmere topcoat to a hat-check girl, and took the elevator to his private office.

Antonio Alvarez was not one of your old-style Mustache Petes. He was an American, born in Miami of Honduran parents. He grew up in the sunburned slums of Hialeah, where the youth gangs hang out under palm trees rather than streetlights. At the age of sixteen he attached himself to Pepito Braga's gang, Los Compañeros de Muerte, a mainly Cuban group dedicated to violent forms of self-betterment. When Braga passed on to his reward, cut down in his prime at the height of a drunken argument with a visiting *machatero* from Guatemala, Alvarez became the right-hand man for Pedro Guitérrez-Flores, the fat, jovial Mexican hitman who for a few years terrorized southern Florida's Central American community for Angel Paz.

Things went along quietly for a while after that, but then trouble erupted among the various underworld factions in the Miami community. Guitérrez was found dead in his car, which was upside down in an irrigation ditch along the Tamiami Trail near 144th Avenue. Accidental death had to be ruled out when the investigating officers ascertained that he had been shotgunned to death and stuffed into the trunk.

And then Angel Paz ended his brief career in treachery and double-dealing hanging upside down from an iron grate in the dungeons of El Malecón after a trip to Havana that didn't work out. Alvarez took note of these changes of fortune and decided life was getting too exciting. Suddenly he wanted security. When the Bahamas Corporation approached him for their gangster-in-residence program, he was more than willing to give up free-lancing in favor of the protection that only a big, well-run corporation can offer. Alvarez was a little man, skinny and dark, with long sideburns which his barber shaped to scimitar points curving toward his well-tended mustache.

He opened the little sliding panel that afforded him a private view of the Tropicabana's stage. A line of chorus girls were doing "Flyin' down to Rio," and he hummed along for a few moments. He took a platinum stashbox out of his pocket and took up the equivalent of a line almost a foot long with a single powerful snort through the hollow ostrich bone he used as a snorter. Then he pushed a buzzer.

Manitas de Córdoba came in, a mournful little man in a heavily starched white guayabera shirt. He worked as a bouncer at the Tropicabana between engagements with Alvarez.

Alvarez explained what needed to be done. Córdoba said he could be ready to roll at once. All they had to do was go to the locker and change into working clothes.

29 • • • • •

It was just after one o'clock that a beat-up Southern Bell telephone repair truck pulled up near Framijian's house. Two men got out, both loaded with equipment, and with leather cases full of pliers dangling from their belts. One of the men adjusted his spikes and climbed the pole. While the other man watched the road, the first man took out a pair of small, powerful binoculars and focused them on Framijian's house. From his position he had a clear view of Framijian's living room, which fronted on the Intracoastal Waterway. The living room's picture window was partly obscured by a venetian blind lowered halfway. The man watched intently for five minutes, then, hearing a warning whistle from his partner, concealed the binoculars and got busy with his tools until the UPS truck had vanished around a turn. Then he watched again, this time for almost fifteen minutes. Then he climbed down.

"What did you see?" Alvarez asked.

"Not much," Córdoba said, "but maybe enough. I saw Framijian."

"You're sure it was him?"

"Sure I'm sure."

"And who else did you see?"

"No one else."

"That's great," Alvarez said. "You did really great."

"But I did see," Córdoba said, "that Framijian was talking to someone."

"Did you get a look at him?"

"No."

"Are you sure somebody else was there?"

"Unless Framijian was rehearsing a speech in front of the mirror."

Alvarez considered it, then shook his head. "No, Framijian never makes no speeches. You done good, Manitas. Let's find a telephone."

PART FOUR

SETTING UP THE KILL

30 • • • • •

The man who arrived at the underground elevator in the Hunt Facility in New Jersey was good-looking, in a florid way. His dark blue suit with the discreet red pinstripe was cut impeccably. His most striking feature was his iron-gray hair, a great bush of it rising above his collar. Another feature worthy of note was his beard, which was spade-shaped and about four inches long. The beard could perhaps be dismissed, since the first thing the newcomer did, once he was inside the Hunt Facility, was to peel it off, fold it carefully, and put it into his small attaché case.

Simmons arrived in the reception area just as the new arrival was snapping the brass clasps on his cordovan briefcase.

"Senator Barenger!" Simmons exclaimed. "How good to see you again! Come to my office."

He led Barenger down a corridor to his office, nicely furnished in greens and dark tans.

"To what do I owe this honor?" Simmons said.

Barenger was still scratching his face, which was irritated from the spirit gum used to hold the false beard in place.

"I'll be glad when these disguises are no longer needed," he commented.

"But for now, it is extremely necessary," Simmons said. "It wouldn't do for anyone to see our famous

Senator from Illinois here in the heart of an illegal organization. Drink, Senator?"

"A nip of Irish would do fine," Barenger said. "Illegal? Yes, the Hunt is still illegal, thanks to the bleeding-heart liberals in Washington. But all that is going to pass, Simmons, you mark my words. Our latest polls show that people all over the country are getting fed up with the situation which permits small, shady-looking people in baggy army discards to blow away innocent citizens. The people of this country want the situation reversed—they want to be the ones doing the blowing away. Legalized murder is an idea whose time has come."

"It's what we are working for," Simmons said. "Meanwhile, legal or not, the Hunt goes on."

"I just came by to check on your progress," Barenger said. "My friends and colleagues, the Free-Murder Congressmen, want to make sure that, even though illegal, the Hunt is proceeding on the agreed-upon rules."

"I can assure you that it is all being done according to your guidelines. But come to the situation room and see for yourself."

Simmons led Barenger out of his office and down a corridor to a large room with rows of computers. Large screens on the wall gave results of various data. A world map had lights flashing on it.

"There's the world Hunt status map," Simmons said. "The original idea was to have one light for each sponsored Hunt. That was all right when we had only twenty or so, but now we have close to five hundred going on at all times. So we represent each ten Hunts in a city by a graded increase in luminosity of the bulb. Over here is the Hunter-to-Victim kill ratio, changed and totalized hourly as new results come in. And here is the special list of non-informed Hunts, directed against terrorists and death-squad leaders, which we are performing as a public service."

Senator Barenger looked over the board with keen interest. His gaze traveled down to Miami, where a single green light was lit.

"What about that one?"

"That's one of our people going after a well-known assassin, Mr. Alfonso Guzmán."

"Glad to see you're getting after that bastard. But what does that yellow light mean that went on just now beside the green light?"

Simmons stared at it. His voice was carefully flat when he said, "The yellow light indicates that a notification has been made to a Victim."

"But I thought you didn't notify the assassins on your list."

"We don't." Simmons was tight-lipped. "Somebody has made a mistake. Excuse me, Senator."

Simmons walked as quickly as dignity would allow to the communications module in a corner of the room. He picked up the annunciator. "Get me Stevens."

The call transfer went through quickly. "Stevens here."

"Stevens, check your file on Hunt 32224A."

"Yes, sir, I've got it. Everything is in order . . . oh, I see."

"The Victim has been notified."

"Yes, sir. I see that."

"How do you explain it? I left explicit orders about that. You know how deadly these professional killers are. Our Hunters don't stand a chance once the professionals are notified."

"I know that, sir. It's either sabotage or human error."

"Who programmed that Hunt?"

"Bwithins, sir. Shall I call him?"

"I'll attend to him. The damage is done. Check all the other Hunts. Double-check. Maybe there's still a chance to rescue this one." He broke the connection, then said to the operator, "Get me Bwithins, Hunt Postal Systems."

They were on a few moments later.

"Message 32241B," Simmons said. "Has it gone out yet?"

"I think it has, sir."

"And been delivered?"

"I don't think so, sir. Not yet."

"Now listen carefully. I want to set up a cancellation on that signal."

"A cancellation? But the letter is on its way."

"This involves the life of one of our Hunters," Simmons said quietly. "You must stop that letter before it reaches its intended person."

"OK, sir," Bwithins said. "I'll do my best. To what degree of severity can I go in structuring this cancellation?"

"All the way to Level 3, the level of the unexplained anomaly," Simmons said.

Bwithins's voice was grim. "Got it, sir. Over and out."

Simmons turned to Barenger. "Senator, I'm glad you noticed that. I only hope we're in time to stop the missive."

"I must be getting back to the Senate cloakroom," Barenger said. "I only wish I could spend more time down here working with you good people. This, in my estimation, is the true home of liberty."

"We'll do our best to live up to that," Simmons said.

After Barenger left, Simmons hurried off to see

the Huntmaster. He burst into the old man's chamber, not bothering with the usual formalities.

"Why?" he asked.

The Huntsmaster's face was amused, imperturbable.

"A cup of tea?" he inquired.

"Don't give me that," Simmons said. "I know you did it. You got Bwithins to send the letter to Guzmán. But why?"

"It was necessary," the Huntmaster said. "To stir things up more."

"Necessary for whom? Certainly not Blackwell!"

The Huntmaster chuckled. "Blackwell will have his hands full, no doubt. But Minska is there to look after him."

"Then why did anyone have to be stirred up?"

"You'll see soon enough. Is our airplane fueled and ready to go?"

"Of course. But where are we going?"

"Don't ask so many questions," the Huntmaster said. "Just stay alert. We'll be going on a moment's notice. Now what about that tea?"

31 •••••

At the big main post office in Newark, at five in the afternoon, a drunken or crazed person managed somehow to get into the locker rooms in area 512. The fire he started there demanded the attention of two brigades of Newark's fire department. When it was over, it was discovered that someone had gotten in and stolen a sack of mail originating from north-central New Jersey.

Bwithins quickly passed the sack of mail through an infrared scanner. The sorting machine whirred noisily, flipping the letters past the hooded snout of the scanner. When the process was done, Bwithins swore. The key document, recognizable by its invisible magnetic coding, had not been in the sack. He telephoned his Miami agent.

Albert Geers had been a postal carrier in South Miami for almost three years. Geers enjoyed driving around in the red-white-and-blue U.S. Postal Service jeep. He had the mail carrier's special resentment of second-class mail, and he was known to carry a spray can of Dog-Gone to take care of contentious canines encountered along his route. But he was in no way remarkable. This rendered all the more mysterious the fact of his disappearance in South Miami, him and his whole sack of mail.

Many theories were put forth. But no one looked at the most telling clue—that Geers had been vanished just after he had delivered the mail to the Guzmán residence.

Even if someone had considered the fact, it would have been useless to his ratiocination except in combination with another fact that the investigators couldn't be expected to deduce from the meager clues at his disposal. That was the fact that someone had tried to prevent the mail from being delivered to Guzmán's place, and had failed by less than five minutes.

32 •••••

"Have a nice day, sir!"

Blackwell tipped the attendant and got into his rented car at the entrance to his hotel. The steering wheel was hot to the touch, but the valet had put on the air conditioning and it was cool inside. He buckled his seat belt, put the car into drive, and went south on Brickell Avenue, past the rows of tall glass and aluminum buildings landscaped with palm trees. He had no trouble following the signs to South Dixie Highway, keeping the elevated Metrorail on his right. The highway ran past Coconut Grove and Coral Gables. When he reached SW 72nd Street he was in South Miami. He found SW 55th Avenue and made a right onto Twin Lakes Drive. At the end of the dead-end street, behind a tall fieldstone fence, he saw a sprawling house behind a high iron fence. He told the man on the gate that he was Frank Blackwell, arriving by invitation, and the man telephoned the main house, got a confirmation, and opened the gate. Blackwell drove up the long, palm-shaded drive to the main house. A very large man with a flat, expressionless face greeted him and pointed to where he could park the car.

Guzmán's home was a coral-pink monstrosity set on a five-acre plot behind a chain-link fence equipped with sensors and guarded by Dobermans. It was known throughout the Hispanic community as Don

Alfonso's Pink Palace, and it was located in South
Miami just past Coral Gables with its tiresome building codes. The house was an anthology of European
styles from Greek Classical through French Chateau
and English Manor to Spanish Colonial with a brief
side trip (the garage, chapel, and stables) to High
Medieval. The Pink Palace was a history of architec-
ture writ small in pink stucco.

Tito opened the front door, patted Blackwell down
quickly and expertly, then led him in. A little maid
in black-and-white uniform was waiting there to es-
cort him the rest of the way. He followed her through
a long entrance hall borrowed from the Borgias
and out the other side to a large kidney-shaped
swimming pool.

On the concrete apron beside the pool a portly
man lay on a lounge chair, his brown hide slick with
suntan lotion and sweat. He wore reflector sunglasses
in a Gucci frame. His face was rectangular, small-
featured, lumpy. He looked like an Indian ironwood
carving.

Alfonso Guzmán was a short, barrel-chested, chest-
nut-brown man with a mat of grizzled gray hair on
his chest. His leathery brown hide glistened with
sweet-smelling tanning lotion. There were three men
sitting with him. One was slender and hawk-faced in
white slacks and white shirt open to the waist. Another was a large, portly, middle-aged man with a
sagging, weary face and a tired mouth beneath a
bandit mustache; he wore a silk bathrobe with a
thunderbird painted on its back. The third man was
young, curly-headed. He smiled an uncertain smile.
To one side was Mercedes, looking cool and lovely in
a pale yellow linen suit.

"Good to see you, Mr. Blackwell. These are my
friends Diego García and Chaco. And this is Mercedes
Brannigan, a friend of the family."

Mercedes smiled at him.

"May we bring you a drink?" Guzmán asked.

"Plain soda and a lot of ice," Blackwell said.

Guzmán snapped his fingers. "Juanito, get it for him, would you?" The slim young man got up, nodded to Blackwell, and went to the bar just inside the overhang.

"Come, let me show you the house," Guzmán said.

Don Guzmán loved his house, because exuberance was his aesthetic and the house fulfilled his need for impressing himself and others. There was the rosewood-paneled den where his friends could admire his collection of guns and hear their histories. Adjoining the den was a target range where Guzmán could show off his considerable skill with anything that fired a projectile. But what he enjoyed most was the big kidney-shaped swimming pool with the comfortable deck chairs and reclining lounges, where he and his friends could drink tall rum drinks and smoke Cuban cigars ("Tobacco has no politics," Guzmán used to say) and talk about the good old days that were gone and the good new days that were coming up.

They returned to poolside. Guzmán said, "Lunch in a few minutes. You want some nose candy? Hey, Juanito, move your ass, *cabrón*, get him a double line of the milky blue Imperial Inca supercrack, and a certified check for a million dollars to snort it up in. You see, amigo, we do things in style around here."

"None for me," Blackwell said. "Not before lunch."

"We'll eat inside," Guzmán said, "in what they call the lanai. I'd like your opinion of my new chef. Ah, here is my wife. Permit me to introduce you."

Caterina Guzmán was a tall, stiff, white-faced lady with strong, unlovely features. She wore a high-necked

gray dress and an ebony crucifix. Her ivory parch-
ment skin proclaimed her scorn for the fun-loving
sun and those who reveled in it. Her appearance cast
a pall on the garlic-wine-tobacco haze of the Latin
good life, reminding the revelers of the uncaring
centuries of death that lay ahead. She pressed
Blackwell's fingers briefly with a cold hand, looked
at him with a cold, fanatic eye, murmured, *"Timor
mortis conturbat me."* And passed on.

"She is very religious," Guzmán said. "Come, let us
eat."

"Will the señora accompany us?" Blackwell asked.

Guzmán shook his head. "She is on one of her
fasts."

Guzmán led the way to the lanai. He reminded
Blackwell a little of an iguana. He looked like a
comedy Central American general high on pictur-
esqueness and low on guts, until Blackwell remembered that this coffee-colored little man with the silly
mustache and the carefully waved iron-gray hair had
commanded the infamous Brigade 432, the Sinver-
güenzas as they were called after the sack of Tun-
buncú. And this same Guzmán had led the Gringitos
de Soledades death squad in Tegucigalpa, and for
three years had been in charge of the infamous
model prison in Managua, the one the United Nations Commission on Human Decency had declared
too foul for objective consideration.

Guzmán might be laughable, but he wasn't negligi-
ble. He was a man who had lived hard and could be
expected to die hard. Blackwell touched the roadmap
in the inside pocket of his seersucker jacket.

The lanai was a long room with latticed jalousies
and a knotty pine entranceway. Guzmán sat in a
big chair at the head of the table, with Blackwell at
his right hand. Mercedes was at his left. Next came

Emilio and Juanito, then two other guests—a Paraguayan professor of economics, small and bearded with heavy horn-rimmed glasses, and his wife, a skinny dark woman with frizzy hair. At the end of the table were Emilio, Diego García, and Chaco.

There was a delicate crab bisque laced with sherry, and then crayfish creole-style, done with garlic, red peppers, and piri-piri sauce, with mango slices on the side. Then jambalaya, served with New Orleans potato puffs and fresh baby corn. There was a light salad enlivened with Gulf shrimp in a rémoulade sauce. The Key lime pie was light, and Blackwell had to push himself to finish a second helping. Then came coffee, brandy, and cigars. After the coffee, the Paraguayan professor and his wife left for their siesta. Emilio and Juanito excused themselves soon after, then García and Chaco. That left just Blackwell, Guzmán, and Mercedes at table. Blackwell felt uncomfortably full, but still capable of making the kill. After he got the check, of course.

Guzmán got up and said to Blackwell, "Come, let's walk in the garden for a few minutes. If you'll excuse us a moment, my dear?"

Blackwell and Guzmán strolled to the ornamental garden beyond the swimming pool. It was a sultry, sleepy Florida afternoon. The sun simmered overhead, bleaching the sky to a faded denim blue. They stopped at the ornamental pond. They stood on a high-peaked little ornamental Japanese bridge. Down below, big goldfish swam lazily back and forth.

"We can talk now," Guzmán said. "When do I get the guns?"

"Tomorrow night," Blackwell said.

"Where?"

"You have a freighter available, I believe?"

"Yes, *El Espíritu de Guanojuato*, taking on fuel in Port Everglades."

"We'll put the guns aboard tomorrow night."

"Where will they come from?"

"That's our business, Mr. Guzmán."

"We've never done business before, Mr. Blackwell," Guzmán said. "I just want you to know that this shipment is very important to me. I have agreed on your price. I want the goods."

"Well, obviously."

"Not entirely obvious, perhaps. There are a lot of unscrupulous people in this town. They'll promise anything. But whether or not they'll let you live to spend the money, that's a different story."

"Is that a threat, Mr. Guzmán?"

"Not at all. Just a warning about some of the people you may encounter down here. Now I suppose you want the money?"

"Mr. Framijian said that was the usual arrangement."

Guzmán reached into his jacket and took out an envelope. He opened it and took out a check. Blackwell saw that it was a certified bearer check for nine million dollars.

"I thought it was supposed to be for twenty," Blackwell said.

"What you have there represents one half of the amount. I'll have the rest for you tomorrow."

"Nine million is not one half of twenty," Blackwell pointed out.

"Naturally, I took my commission," Guzmán said. "Is not the workman worthy of his hire?"

Blackwell hadn't heard about any commission, or any half-now-half-later arrangement. Should he kill Guzmán now or later? Well, it was time he got this show on the road. He folded the check and put it into an inside jacket pocket.

"Well, I've got to go," he said. "Sorry to eat and run, but there's a lot to do."

"Of course, I understand. You come back tomorrow night. I'm throwing a big party, lots of food, drugs, women, music, laughs. I'll have the rest of the money then."

"OK," Blackwell said. "Perhaps you could help me out on some map directions." He took the poisoned roadmap out of his pocket.

"Of course. Where do you want to go?" Guzmán asked, reaching for the roadmap.

"The Seaquarium," Blackwell said. "I hear they got dolphins there. I'm crazy about dolphins."

Before Guzmán could grasp the map, another hand reached into the frame and took the roadmap. The hand was wearing a long white glove. Mercedes's hand.

"The Seaquarium? You must have passed it when you came out here from Miami. Here it is, right here. Are you really interested in fish, Mr. Blackwell?"

"Oh, yes," Blackwell said hastily. "But mainly it's the dolphins I'm interested in."

"I was going there myself," Mercedes said. "You could follow me in your car."

"Hey, great," Blackwell said. He was somewhat relieved that he didn't have to make the kill right at this moment. Anyhow, Minska would probably have scolded him for not waiting and picking up the other nine million tomorrow night.

Deftly he retrieved the roadmap from her. They walked together to their cars.

33 • • • • •

The maid cleared away the lunch and cleaned up. Emilio watched the operation, then went for the mail. It was on the little mahogany table in the entrance hall beside the hollowed-out elephant foot where the umbrellas were kept. He looked it over. There was the usual collection of bills. They could go to Juanito. There were appeals from political candidates and announcements of new restaurants opening. Junk mail. And there was one letter in a heavy vellum envelope, cream-colored, somehow official-looking even though, European-style, it did not have a return address. Emilio, Guzmán's death-squad lieutenant from the bad old days, now working as Guzmán's batman, picked up the envelope between a calloused thumb and a blackened forefinger. Some vague presentiment of disaster must have come to the grizzled veteran, because he shook himself once, like a wet dog, and thrust out his lower lip. Then he brought the letter to Guzmán.

Don Alfonso sat in the big Barcalounger in his den nursing a hangover, a swollen nose, and inflamed sinuses. He picked up the cream-colored envelope and frowned at it. Then, taking a trench knife from his desk, he slit open the letter and read the contents.

"This is your official notification of Victim status in Hunt 23441a.

"Good luck,

"The Hunt Committee."

"Emilio!" Guzmán bellowed.

Emilio hurried in from the hall where he had been waiting patiently for Guzmán to bellow for him.

"Read this," Guzmán said, "and tell me what you make of it."

34 • • • • •

Alvarez, on the car phone, said, "You're calling from where?"

"The Seaquarium," Mercedes said. "It's the first chance I've had to get away. What's happening?"

"Nobody's made a move yet. Framijian is inside the house, I've seen him a couple times, and I'm pretty sure somebody's in there with him, but I don't know who yet. Manitas is up on the phone pole trying to see in. We're taking turns. Listen, I'm out of cigarettes, and there's no place within a mile of here to get any. How long am I supposed to stay here?"

"Until we figure out what's going on," Mercedes said.

"How long is that going to take? I've got a date tonight."

"Forget it. The Bahamas Corporation pays you plenty for the little use they make of you. You stay there until whoever's in there comes out."

Alvarez put down the phone. He cursed to himself. How could he have forgotten to put an extra carton of cigarettes in the glove compartment? And how about his date tonight with Lola Montez?

Motion down the street caught his eye. He saw a woman walking toward Framijian's house. He was sure she was going to pass, but no, she turned in, went to the door.

Alvarez wondered who the hell that could be.

35 • • • • •

"Knock with eight," Framijian said. He put down his cards with a jingle. The jingle was from the chain that ran from his handcuffs to the table leg.

"Son of a bitch!" Minska said. "How you catch me like that all the time?"

"Hey, listen, babe," Framijian said, "I'm from Miami, we got the best rummy players in the world here. But you're really not bad at all."

"Thanks a lot," Minska said. "That's four hundred I owe you."

"Six hundred. We were doubling down the last hand, don't you remember?"

"I'm getting sleepy," Minska said. "What is it, twenty hours since I got any sleep?"

"This man of yours, you sure he's reliable?"

"Of course he is. But he's new. Not an old pro like us."

"Well, I just hope so. Why hasn't he called? Your life is on the line here too, you know, just as much as mine. How long you think my friends are going to be put off with weirdo excuses like I have to stay here alone and take care of my gout?"

"That's exactly the sort of weirdo reason for staying alone that friends respect. Believe me, I'm an expert in holding people captive."

"OK, if you say so," Framijian said. "Look, why don't you let me bribe you and we can both stop this horsing around and do something more interesting. A million one hundred thou. And the undying friendship of Yitzhak Framijian. Can't say fairer than that, can I?"

"It's a very nice offer," Minska said, "and I want you to know I appreciate it. But I'm sorry, I can't take it."

"Why not?"

"Because I'm an old-fashioned inner-directed kind of person," Minska said with dignity.

"Just my luck," Framijian said. "Wanna play again?"

"Sure. Your deal."

"I can't deal so good with these cuffs on."

"You're doing fine," Minska said.

Framijian reached for the cards, then stopped. Both men sat rigidly still. They had heard an ominous sound: a key in the lock.

"Who has a key to this place?" Minska demanded.

"No one. Unless it's—"

The door flew open. In marched a small, busty red-headed lady in a Kelly-green playsuit and three-inch wedgies.

"Rosalie!" Framijian cried.

"I just couldn't stay away from you any longer," Rosalie said. "You know I still love you, ya big lug. Who's this guy?"

"Just a friend," Framijian said.

"If he's a friend, why are you wearing handcuffs?"

"Because we're playing a game."

"I see," Rosalie said. "Aren't you glad to see me?"

"Rosalie, baby, I'm overjoyed. You know how I've been begging you to return! But the thing is, it's a little awkward just now. I wish you'd called first. I mean, I'm trying to conduct a little business."

"In handcuffs?"

"Forget about the handcuffs, we're just playing a game. Where's Hannah?"

"With my parents."

"Give her my love. I gotta finish up this business, love, and then we'll get together."

"You said we could have a new life if I came back!"

"We're going to. But first I have to finish up this business."

"But that's how it was in the old life!"

"Rosalie, will you please get out of here?"

Rosalie was puzzled. This wasn't like Framijian. He always let her stay around when he discussed business. She looked the new man up and down. Big, lumpy, not very nice-looking. And there was something about him. Yes, he looked dangerous. And she was starting to think there was something a little ominous about the handcuffs, too. What kind of games do grown men play in handcuffs?

Something was going on, and Rosalie suddenly realized that she should have realized that about five minutes earlier.

In the comprehension game it's always better late than never.

"Well, nice to meet you, Mr. whatever-your-name-is," she said. "I'm sorry I came at a bad time. I'll come back later."

Minska had made up his mind. "No, come on in, Rosalie. I don't suppose we can play rummy anymore, but maybe you know hearts? That's a good three-handed game."

"Hey," Rosalie said. "What are you talking about?"

Then she saw the gun in his hand.

There was a moment of respectful silence for the gun.

Then Rosalie said, "You sure you wouldn't want

me to just forget I ever walked in here? It'll make it a lot simpler for you, and I'd never say or do anything that would hurt Framijian."

"Sit down, Rosalie," Minska said.

Rosalie looked at Framijian. He shrugged and smiled sheepishly. She looked at Minska. He looked like the kind of bastard who would shoot a lady.

She came into the living room and sat down. "I shoulda listened to my mother," she said to Minska. "Stay away from that guy, she told me, he's due for an early and spectacular death. But no, I have to get sentimental."

"Rosalie, it'll work out all right," Framijian said.

"Do you play hearts?" Minska asked.

"No," she said. And sighed. And then smiled, a little wanly, but a smile all the same. "But I can learn."

Rosalie was excitable, but she was a good sport.

36 • • • • •

The telephone rang. Framijian answered it as he had been instructed to do.

"Framijian here."

"I'd like to speak to the other fellow," Blackwell said.

"What?"

"The other fellow who's in there with you."

"Who are you?"

"I'm the man who was with him last night."

"Oh, that fellow. Well, your friend has stepped out for a pizza, said he'd be right back."

Blackwell's mind reeled. Had Minska gone crazy? Then he heard a loud sound over the phone, like the sound of a wise guy being slapped on the side of the head, and Minska was on the line saying, "How are you doin', kid? Didn't make the kill, huh?"

"Wasn't able to. But I'll get another chance tomorrow at this party Guzmán is throwing."

"Where are you now?"

"I'm in Coconut Grove with this lady named Mercedes. I think she may be involved in this, so I figured I'd better check her out."

"I guess you might as well," Minska said. "You got nothing to do until tomorrow night. I'll just go on playing hearts here with Framijian and Rosalie."

"Who's Rosalie?"

"Framijian's wife. Hell of a time she picked for a reconciliation, huh?"

"So what's the plan?"

"Meet me at eight o'clock at my room at the Nemo. We'll discuss final arrangements."

37 • • • • •

Blake and Coelli came into the Federal Building for the Fifth District at 346 W. Flagler.

Miss Eustachio at the reception desk flipped open the intercom. "They're here, sir," she said.

"Send them in," Dickerson said, betraying his annoyance by his attempt to keep his voice neutral. He put his newly arrived copy of *Southern Antique Collector* in the top drawer of his Lucite-and-ironwood desk. This was serious.

Dickerson was the new district director for CIA Field Operations, Florida South, extending from Fort Lauderdale to Key West. He was a big man who always wore white suits and a snap-brim panama hat. His agents had a bet on as to what movie role he was acting out. Blake thought he was playing the Walter Huston role from *The Treasure of Sierra Madre,* where Humphrey Bogart panhandles this guy having his shoes shined and it turns out to be Huston, who flips him a silver dollar and asks him to kindly panhandle someone else next time. And with that silver dollar Bogart buys a lottery ticket and wins a small prize next day, and that gives him enough money to go into the mountains looking for gold with Tim Holt and Walter Huston and end up macheted to death within sight of town and safety.

Dickerson carried a silver dollar, and sometimes flipped it up and down in a meditative way when he was trying to come to some important decision, like where to have lunch.

No one would ever know if he was fantasizing the Walter Huston role, however, because no one was intimate enough with the district director to ask him.

Dickerson was not a man who invited intimacies.

He said, "What do you know about Alfonso Guzmán?"

Dickerson was new in this station. He had recently been transferred from Phoenix, where he'd had to learn a long list of Spanish names in order to stay on top of activities in the area. Here in Miami he had to learn a whole new list of Spanish names, as well as the usual list of Anglo names, plus some Haitian names.

"Guzmán is one of our friends, sir. One of Somoza's old Guardia Nacional. He still has contacts with the anti-Sandinista guerrilla groups in Central America. Buys arms for them."

"With our assistance?"

"Well, of course, sir," Blake said. "It was the policy of your predecessor, Mr. Bradford, who was, I believe, under direct orders from someone with a direct line to the White House. Might I inquire, sir," asked Blake, "if there's some difficulty about Guzmán?"

"That's what I'm trying to figure out," Dickerson said. "I've just had a call from the Guzmán house."

"From Guzmán himself, sir?"

"No, from some kid who said he was calling from a phone booth. But of course we've had his phone tapped. Or rather, my predecessor had his phone ‛apped and I hadn't gotten around to taking it out."

"What did this person say?" Blake asked.

"He wanted to talk to you. One of your informants, no doubt. I said that you weren't here but that he could talk to me."

"I don't mean to be critical, sir, but no one is supposed to talk to an agent's informants except the agent himself."

"If said agent happened to be around to get his call. Why don't you carry a beeper?"

"I do, sir," Blake said. "But I've been changing services. Phoneswift has been screwing up my messages so I've gone over to PhonoTel. Juanito must have called just before they turned on my service."

"He didn't leave his name," Dickerson said.

"It must have been Juanito, Guzmán's nephew. He's the only informant I've got in the house. What did he say, sir, if I may inquire?"

"He said that his uncle had just received a very strange letter. From some group that call themselves the Hunt Committee. They told Guzmán that he's going to be a Victim in some Hunt. Blake, do you know anything about this?"

"I've heard of the Hunt Corporation, sir."

"Some sort of vigilante organization?"

"Not quite like that, sir. They've been characterized as the libertarians of murder. They represent the so-called extreme-left-wing anarchist-liberal attitude toward murder. So I'm told. If they exist, sir."

"Well, *do* they exist?"

"Perhaps not, sir. It's almost a ludicrous notion, this idea of the Hunters. But then the Mafia is a sort of silly idea, too—who could imagine a bunch of old-country Sicilians running all the important unions in the United States, controlling the ports, trucking, to say nothing of prostitution and gambling, even making secret deals with the United States at the time of the Sicily landings in World War Two."

"Then you think we should take this Hunt seriously?"

"I think we must, sir. The officials who claimed there was no such thing as the Mafia are no longer employed. They rendered themselves obsolete because of their rigid belief structure."

"Like the dodo," Coelli said.

"What?" said Dickerson.

"Obsolete bird," Coelli said, looking embarrassed, like a man who had been caught dreaming with his eyes open. "I mean, I think there's a parallel, sir."

Dickerson looked at Blake. Blake said, "Analogy may not be Coelli's strong point, but he's the best we've got in fieldcraft."

"No doubt," Dickerson said. "Well then, we'll act on the assumption that the Hunt is real, though illegal, and the Hunters, whoever they are, have sent an assassin out to kill Alfonso Guzmán. We don't want Guzmán dead, do we, Blake?"

"I wouldn't think so, sir. We want to keep the contras supplied. They're a bunch of bastards, but they're our bastards. To supply them we're best off going through Guzmán. It saves us the cost of setting up our own liaison with the guerrillas and arranging our own drops. That policy was dropped after the fiasco in 1986, sir, if you remember."

"Of course I remember," Dickerson said. "I was opposed to the whole thing from the beginning."

"So was I, sir," Blake said. "It was really all the fault of your predecessor, who must have misinterpreted something someone close to the White House said to him. We don't want that again. The way it looks now, the political future of Nicaragua and maybe all Central America may depend on this one, and we will look very silly if our candidate isn't in the capital with the rest of them when V-Day or whatever they call it finally comes."

"No one told me about all this," Dickerson said. "I wish someone had filled me in on the situation beforehand."

"There was no need for you to know beforehand," Blake said.

"But I'm district director!"

"Do you know how many district directors have been found out to be double agents in the last ten years?"

"Blake, if you're implying—"

"I'm not, sir! I'm just pointing out that there have been a lot of leaks lately and everybody's been requested to be extra-tight with information and give it out only on a need-to-know basis."

"All right. The situation is beginning to clarify. There are arms going to the contras through Guzmán."

Blake made a gesture with his head that could have been interpreted as a nod.

"This is going to be the big one for the contras."

This time Blake blinked twice, a possible sign of agreement.

"But there's a Hunter involved in this," Blake mused.

"So it seems," Dickerson agreed.

"Since you've just come down from Washington," Blake said, "maybe you know what the new policy is toward the Hunt?"

"Maybe I do," Dickerson said. He didn't want to admit that he hadn't even met the new chief, didn't know his name, and was allowed to communicate with him only by telephone after an elaborate recognition code had been exchanged. He looked at Blake fixedly for a few moments, and Blake began to feel uncomfortable. Finally he said, "Listen, Blake, you're one of the old ideological people, am I correct? From the last Congress, I mean. Back when you secret service types had conviction. Essentially, that is?"

"I suppose you could call me ideological," Blake said. "I did have some favorites. But I'm flexible. Expediency is my motto."

"I thought you might feel that way. That's why I can still use you. There have been a lot of changes recently."

"Yes sir."

"I'm a new appointee. I can keep whom I want and fire whom I want in this department."

"Yes, sir."

"The thing to remember, Blake, is that we're not doing ideology any more. Not in this administration. What you did do was fine, I suppose. I don't know much about it or care. It was ideological and that's not what we're interested in anymore. Just don't do things for ideological reasons anymore."

"Yes sir. What is the new reason?"

"The new administration is interested in pragmatism and cost accounting."

"Sir?"

"Whatever we do, whatever any agency of the government does, it has to show a profit."

"That's only sensible."

"And it also follows that we put forth our best efforts in what is going to bring in the best return."

"Of course, sir. I'm all in favor of this course, sir. I've always believed that fiscal responsibility is the only road to happiness."

"This agency, too, is going to show a profit."

"Of course. That's the new secret directive, isn't it, sir? I just wanted to be absolutely sure I understood. I can work with that, sir. And frankly, it's not entirely unprecedented. We used to work for a profit back in the last administration, at least some of the time."

"Maybe you did," Dickerson said. "But not to the extent we're going to do it now. Nobody's followed the doctrine of profit to its simple conclusion."

"What do you want me to do about the Hunter?"

"Find out who he is, keep him under surveillance, but don't hurt him. At least not yet, until I've gotten further orders."

38 • • • • •

Mercedes had settled into a small house owned by the Bahamas Corporation in the middle of a miniature jungle of banana trees, cabbage palms, several varieties of epiphytes, and a majestic old banyan tree. The little house had a screened porch running around two sides. The windows were curtained in red gingham. There were two rocking chairs on the porch, and an old-fashioned glider. The place was shaded by tropical trees, shaded and silent except for the loud hum of hard-bodied insects.

"Why don't you sit in the rocker?" Mercedes asked. "I'll mix up something cool. Rum punch OK?"

Blackwell leaned back in the rocker. It creaked comfortably. He settled his feet on the rail that ran around the room, setting his heels on top of the scuff marks that showed that others had had the same idea. He clasped his hands behind his head and leaned back. He sighed. The heat was intense, and he felt drained, but not uncomfortable, peaceful, in fact, and that was rare for him. There was a moist, fertile, decaying sort of odor in the air. Florida was the sort of place that always seemed to be threatening to slip out of time and go back to the Paleozoic where it belonged. The light was a tawny gold filtered through a fragmented wall of green.

Mercedes came back in a few minutes with two frosted tulip glasses filled with reddish-yellow rum

175

punch. She had mixed them cold and tart, a little like herself, and Blackwell sipped. The golden afternoon drifted into the violet hues of evening.

Some hours later, Mercedes asked Blackwell, "What do you do when you're not selling guns?"

Blackwell arranged her head more comfortably on his shoulder. They were lying propped up on pillows in Mercedes's big double bed. Just one small light was on in the living room. It was just past midnight. Against the shaded window black palm silhouettes bowed to each other.

"Can you keep a secret?"

"Sure."

"I teach karate in New York."

39 •••••

On the television screen, Clint Eastwood said, "Go ahead, make my day."

"That's the line," Framijian said. "I always love that line. 'Make my day.' That's what I call tough. Right, baby?"

Rosalie, droopy-eyed in the big armchair, said, "Honey, it's a wonderful line, but I've already heard it about three times tonight."

"Well, it's still good," Framijian said. "What about you, stranger? You like that line?"

Minska was sitting in the wing chair, his eyelids drooping. It was three-twenty in the morning. Minska had lost count of when he had slept last. He roused himself, stretched, yawned. "Yeah, it's a good line," he said. "But enough movies."

"You wanna play some more rummy?"

Minska shook his head. "I think it's time we got some sleep."

"Hey, that's a real good idea, sport," Framijian said. "Do you want to take the guest bedroom? It's got one of those Japanese futon beds, best sleeping you'll ever get. Rosie and I'll flop down in the main bedroom. How does that sound?"

"It sounds like you think I'm pretty dumb," Minska said.

Framijian raised both his hands palm upward. An

imploring gesture. "Hey, you got me wrong. I never think the man with the gun is dumb. I respect guns, I'm in the business myself."

"He didn't mean anything by it," Rosalie said. She was pretty sleepy herself. She only hoped that Framijian wasn't going to try anything. This big guy looked like he was thinking a couple steps ahead all the time. She had the feeling he wasn't going to kill them if they did what he said. She wasn't sure, but she thought so. She thought it was a better bet than trying to tackle him here in the house. But the question was, what did Framijian think?

"So what do you propose?" Framijian asked, yawning. It had been a big day for everybody.

"You two will sleep here on the couch, where I can see you," Minska said. He took out the handcuffs key. "Now stay very still. I'm going to have to do this one-handed so I can keep the gun in the other hand. Don't make me think you're going for my gun."

Left-handed, he unlocked Framijian's handcuffs. The MAG 50 was in his right hand. His finger rested lightly but definitively on the trigger. Framijian didn't move a hair as Minska handcuffed him and Rosalie together.

"Comfortable?" he asked.

"Well, it's cozy," Framijian said. "Right, baby?"

"I just wish I could lie down," Rosalie said.

"Sorry," Minska said. "That's too difficult to arrange. Now there's just one final thing."

He took out his bag, rummaged through it for a moment, and came up with a device that looked like an alarm clock. He pressed buttons, set it, and then put it on the side of the couch beside Framijian.

"What's that?" Framijian asked.

"Little antipersonnel bomb. The booby-trap model. It's set to disarm itself in twelve hours."

"Oh. But why did you put it here?"

"It's got a little rocker device inside," Minska said. "Sets it off if it's knocked over or anything. That's so you'll stay nice and quiet on the couch, not go rummaging around in the upholstery for maybe a hidden gun or a grenade."

"I haven't got any hidden guns!" Framijian said.

"Maybe so, maybe not. I haven't got the time to search this whole place. This just makes sure you'll stay still."

Framijian protested. But Minska had made up his mind. He went across the room and lay down on the rug. He set his small wrist alarm and lay down with the MAG 50 under his cheek. He was asleep almost at once.

After a while Framijian said, "Do you think he's bluffing?"

"About what?"

"About that thing being a booby trap. I never heard of any trap shaped like that, and I ought to know."

"Is it worth risking our lives to find out?" Rosalie asked.

"Almost. I'd give a lot to turn the tables on that son of a bitch."

"Not with me on this couch too," Rosalie said, her voice going up in panic.

"Don't worry, I'm not going to do anything."

An intermittent sound came from Minska. It sounded a little like a death rattle, only lower and in shorter bursts.

"The son of a bitch is snoring," Framijian said. "Dammit, I don't see how we can sleep like this. Rosalie, you hear me?"

A soft bubbling sound came from Rosalie. She was a ladylike snorer.

"Christ," Framijian said, with feeling. He settled back on the couch, making his movements very light and even. He was still thinking about how he could never sleep like this when he fell asleep.

PART FIVE

THE BIG CHASE

40 • • • • •

Emilio hadn't known what to think of the letter from the Hunt people, but he had known what to do about it. He had telephoned Barnes Associates in the Federal Building on Lincoln Mall in Miami Beach. They handled a lot of Guzmán's legal business. Guzmán was a valuable client. They said it wasn't their usual line, but they'd look into it and call back in the morning. They called promptly at nine. After talking to them, Emilio went to see Guzmán in the den.

"All right," Guzmán said. "What have you found out?"

"Barnes Associates tells me there's a game called Killer which is played on college campuses. It is based on a short story by Robert Sheckley called 'The Seventh Victim,' and a film of that story called *The Tenth Victim*."

"Yes, I saw the movie," Guzmán said. "On the late television. It is a silly story about a woman hunting a man in Rome and they fall in love. Something like that. But that's fantasy, Emilio."

"No," Emilio said. "It is real. The game, I mean. College students play it all over America. With water guns and bags of flour. It's been going on for more than twenty years."

"So what?"

"There's a whole generation has played this Killer

game. Suppose some of them got the idea of doing it for real?"

"But that would be crazy!"

"With respect," Emilio said, "I must remind you that what we did at Encantado was crazy, too, and so was Santa Inez and Number 61."

"Don't remind me," Don Alfonso said. "Those were savage times."

"And what about now? The situation is much the same. And consider your own line of work, Don Alfonso. Would you ever have believed you would become a killer of political dissidents far from home?"

"It's not what I would have chosen," Guzmán said. "But a man puts his hand to what work comes his way. I always did a good clean job."

"When you were head of the model prison, you tortured people."

"Of course I did. Torturing people is part of a Central American prison commander's job, and therefore one does it cleanly, which in this case means thoroughly."

"Some people would still consider it crazy," Emilio said.

"That's because they haven't been there," Guzmán said firmly.

"I'm just saying, Don Alfonso, that in the context of our lives and our experience, this Hunt Corporation going around killing people isn't so strange a concept. I mean, there are many groups killing people for one reason or another, why not for the Hunt Corporation's reasons? They're no crazier than some. A lot saner, in fact, when one considers the increasing radicalization of the entire world population—"

Guzmán held up his hand. "Spare me a repetition of your views, Emilio. You were thrown out of the CPN for catastrophism and negativism."

"True enough. But, *mi comandante*, I beg of you to take this warning seriously, even though these people may be crazies. Since the invention of gunpowder, crazies have been bad news."

Guzmán didn't need Emilio to tell him that. He was still thinking about it when Dr. Machado-Ropas called that afternoon. Guzmán had forgotten that it was time for his six-month checkup.

Dr. Machado-Ropas was a small plump man in his early sixties with a goatee and tinted lenses.

When he had finished the examination and closed his bag, Machado-Ropas said bluntly, "What's worrying you, Don Alfonso?"

"Nothing, nothing," Guzmán said. "How are my tests?"

"Assuming the lab reports are all right, you're fine. But your blood pressure is significantly elevated. That's a dangerous sign in a man like you. Can't you tell me what's wrong? I'm your family doctor. I'd like to help."

"There's nothing you can do. I have a little trouble. Nothing I can't handle."

"Have you had any important changes in your life recently?"

"Not really. Well, there is a new man I'm dealing with."

"A new man? Is he reliable?"

"I'm not sure. There's something strange about him."

"And this has been upsetting you?"

"Yes, I suppose it has been."

"Then I beg you, my dear Don Alfonso, kill this person and rid your mind of this anxiety."

"You think it's so easy," Guzmán asked, "just to kill anyone who might be upsetting you?"

"I didn't say it was easy. Its ease or difficulty is no concern of mine. I merely advised you as your doctor to remove the source of anxiety."

"I don't need my doctor to tell me to get rid of people dangerous to me. That would be like asking my lawyer to advise me about my haircuts."

"I fail to see the connection," Dr. Machado-Ropas said.

"You are a literalist, doctor," Guzmán said. "I like that in my medical man. For you, my health should be the thing itself, not a metaphor for something else. Forgive me for using a figure of speech in your presence, old friend. And yes, I will take care of this person as soon as it is convenient and I have the time."

"That's what you always say about smoking, too," the doctor said. But he was smiling indulgently. He had known Guzmán a very long time. Since childhood. All one's friends and enemies came from childhood. And all of one's clients, too.

Alfonso Guzmán selected a Montecristo No. 1, carefully set fire to it, and settled back for a few moments of interior monologue.

I made the choices that I had to make. It was the spirit of the times. I have nothing to be ashamed of. But I protest too much; I don't believe myself; I know the signs; I've had too much experience at spotting a guilty conscience. All of them confess at the end, when the pain is too great to bear. But the honesty of a man demands that he take one hard look at his difficulties and then put them away forever and go on living, because that is being a man. But look at it, because that is being a man. I had to do what I did. And yes, there came a time when I no longer had to do it. I could have, as they say, hung up the gun. But it was all I knew how to do. And to desist from murdering my enemies would lay a reproach upon my friends, acknowledging my regret for what we've done all these years. And I don't consider it wrong. It's too complicated; I can't explain it; history may condemn us, but we were not wrong. It's not so simple; you're born into a certain way of life; you have your friends and your enemies, what are you to do—declare yourself morally diseased and put yourself under house arrest at the north pole?

Guzmán explained the situation to Emilio. Emilio said, "What do you want to do about it, boss? Want me to find this guy Blackwell and turn out his light?"

"Not so fast," Guzmán said. "You've heard the old Chinese saying, 'Softly, softly, catchee monkey'?"

Emilio thought about it. At last he figured it out. "You want I should use the silencer?"

"No, no," Guzmán said.

"Is there a monkey mixed up in this?" Emilio asked.

"Forget about the old Chinese saying. We're going to go through with this exactly as planned."

"But boss! This guy is maybe planning to kill you! I don't see what's in it for you."

"I'll tell you what's in it for me," Guzmán said. "There's Miguelito, the success of our cause, and a very good profit on this arms transaction."

"You think he's going to deliver?"

"Yes, I do."

"What makes you think so?"

"Because Framijian is setting it up. Framijian always comes through."

"But maybe they've gotten to Framijian."

"That doesn't matter. That's not my concern.

Framijian is backed by the Bahamas Corporation. Their representative, Miss Brannigan, is here on the scene. They are guaranteeing this operation. I'd look pretty silly if I backed out now just because some crank sent me a letter, wouldn't I? They'd say, 'Guzmán is getting to be like an old woman—we'd better not do business with him anymore.' We wouldn't like that, would we?"

"No," Emilio said, considering it. "But we wouldn't like getting killed, either."

"Forewarned is forearmed."

"Is that another old Chinese saying, boss?"

"What I'm trying to tell you, Emilio, is that we are going to do everything as planned. With only one difference. Before this Blackwell can make a move, if he's going to make a move, we are going to take him down hard."

"Ah," said Emilio. "That I can understand. That's like the old days."

Guzmán's eyes went misty for a moment. "The old days, back in Central America! When I was El Terror Blanco and you were Sergeant Muerte Tarde!"

"Good days, boss," Emilio said.

"We shall not see their like again, old friend. But this should be an interesting time this evening."

41 •••••

After leaving the district director's office, Blake went straight to a telephone booth and made an urgent telephone call to Johnny Romero. Romero was his main undercover subagent in Miami's Latin community. Blake described Blackwell briefly and told Romero that he had to know where he was, and mentioned that he needed the information faster than instantaneously. He asked him to call back at the public phone at the Rexall on SW 8th and 17th.

Johnny Romero passed the word throughout the collections of barrios that dot the Greater Miami area like infestations of Central Americanitis, the disease by which gray people turn brown, brown coffee turns black, potatoes are replaced by frijoles, beef gives way to pork, and the police inherit the earth. The word was passed—find Blackwell—to the multifarious inhabitants of the southern Florida cities of the swamplands. The Columbians, drinking black coffee in a narrow, neon-lit cafeteria on SW 21st Avenue, heard the news and told the Guatemalans, drinking pulque and listening to Andean harp music in the back of a numbers place where South Dixie Highway intersects with Bird Avenue. One of the Guatemalans knew a Nicaraguan from Isabella la Vieja—they were cousins, in fact—and he asked him. This Nicaraguan, Danillo Tomasillo, who worked as a night porter at the Turfrider, considered the news carefully, then went into a bolita parlor disguised as a mom-and-pop grocery and made a call to Johnny Romero. Romero telephoned Blake and said he'd be right over.

"You know something about these Hunters, don't you?" Coelli asked when Blake came out of the telephone booth.

They were on the corner of SW 8th Street and 17th Avenue in front of the Rexall as Latinity in its many forms danced, pranced, minced, and limped past to the rhythms of hi-fi salsa blaring out of the loudspeakers of competing hi-fi stores. The effect was reminiscent of that scene in *Spellbound* where the fantasy begins to fade and everything blares and honks discordantly, threatening momentarily to dissolve into some other reality. The reality of SW 8th was stretched to the limit, but it never quite popped.

"Indeed I do," Blake said. "I didn't mention it to Dickerson, but there was a special briefing last month in Tallahassee, just before you arrived." He paused. "You've got a double-A priority security clearance, isn't that right?"

Coelli nodded.

"Maybe I'd better see about getting you a triple-A. This information is not for circulation below that."

"For Chrissakes!" Coelli said. "I'm your partner! I need to know this stuff in case you get knocked down during some part of an operation and I have to take over."

"All right," Blake said. "I suppose I have to trust you." You could see it didn't come easily. "The Hunt is real. We have reason to believe that many more Hunts—as they call their assassinations—will be made."

Coelli was munching on a sulfur-yellow cuchifrito

when Johnny Romero pulled up in his yellow Ford convertible with the red racing stripe down the side.

"What's up?" Blake asked.

"A party," Romero said. "That's where Blackwell's going to be tonight."

"We're on our way."

42 • • • • •

Blackwell looked around an unfamiliar bedroom. There seemed to be a lot of clothing lying on the floor. Most of it was woman's clothing. Some of it was his. He seemed to be lying naked in somebody's bed. From the long shadows outside, he figured it was late afternoon.

Mercedes's voice called out from the other room. "Hey, you awake yet? Coffee?"

"Yes, please, yes," Blackwell said. She came over to his bed with the steaming mug. She was wearing a pale green playsuit made of some nubby material. She looked good enough to box up and ship to yourself at some address in the desert or high mountains for days of uninterrupted rutting and nights of howling at the moon.

While Blackwell dressed, Mercedes quickly straightened up the kitchen. She had managed, during the course of the night and morning, to examine every inch of his clothing and body. A telltale label from Bamberger's in Newark tended to confirm his admission that he was either a resident of New Jersey or had visited there recently. His weapons had been good; the Rolex gun was especially nice, and she was planning to ask the Bahamas Corporation to make one up for her. But who was he working for?

Blackwell looked at his watch. "Hey, time I got

back to my hotel. I've got a few things to do before the party."

"I've got a few things to take care of, too. I'll see you there."

He'd turned out to be a lot more fun than she'd anticipated. Something to do with body chemistry, no doubt. One of those uncanny clicks that she read about in romance novels but never had experienced before. Nor expected to. She'd been lucky she hadn't told him everything about herself during some of the finer moments of their joint sexual performance, especially the weird business with the octopi and the sushi that she blushed to think about now.

She still didn't know who he worked for. At climactic moments you just don't say, "Honey, just who in the hell are you, really?"

Mercedes waited until she heard the sound of his car start up and drive away. Then she poured herself another cup of coffee and called Alvarez.

43 •••••

It was getting toward evening. Golden sunset lighting streamed through the cracks in the venetian blinds on Framijian's living-room windows. Minska was dressed now in lightweight slacks and a Hawaiian sports shirt. He finished packing his underwater gear into a cheap plastic tote bag. On the couch, handcuffed together, Framijian and Rosalie watched him make his preparations. They were both aware that this was the most dangerous moment. What would he do with them before he left?

"You're probably wondering what I'm going to do with you when I leave," Minska said.

"No, not at all," Framijian said, with a confidence he didn't feel. "We've cooperated with you all the way. And I've promised that we won't say or do a thing for twenty-four hours. We're handcuffed together here on the couch. Can't move, can't do a thing. So it's OK, isn't it?"

Minska took out a long knife with a razor-sharp hollow-ground edge.

"Hey, please!" Rosalie said.

"Sorry, lady. I have to do this." Minska crossed the room and cut the telephone wires. Then he looked at Framijian and Rosalie thoughtfully.

"Now what's the matter?" Framijian asked.

"I was just wondering if you might not have a set

of picks hidden around here somewhere. For all I know you could be out of those cuffs five minutes after I'm gone."

"Hey!" Framijian said, genuinely outraged. "I gave you my word I'd just sit here for twenty-four hours!"

"Still," Minska said, "what else could you say under the circumstances? I guess I need another precaution, just as a precaution."

Minska opened his bag, rummaged in it, found a smaller bag, opened it. He took out an object about the size of a pack of king-size filter cigarettes. The object was made of black metal and had two dials and two switches. Minska turned one of the switches, set the dials, walked over to Framijian and Rosalie with the little machine in his hand, set it on the sofa cushion, and flipped the other switch.

Rosalie began to wail. Framijian started to splutter.

"Don't worry, nothing's going to happen," Minska said. "This is just insurance. You'll both be OK as long as you stay still."

"What is it?" Framijian asked.

"Small bomb. Different type from the one I used last night. This one is armed with C27. It'll disarm itself in twenty-four hours if you don't set it off beforehand."

"What do we do in order not to set it off?" Framijian asked.

"It has a motion-sensitive pendulum caged in a conductive cone. You're OK as long as you sit still. But if you move around, shake the cushions, the thing goes off. It's called the Immobility-Maker."

"Wait a minute!" Framijian said. "What if one of us sneezes?"

"A light sneeze is probably OK," Minska said.

"You can't just leave us here like this!" Framijian throated.

"It's better than being dead," Minska said, "which is what you would be if I weren't ethical."

He left, closing the door quietly behind him.

44 •••••

The doorbell chimed again. Framijian had the sort of doorbell that plays chimes. He had long planned to have it changed. But you know how it is when you're busy. He looked at Rosalie, managing to do so by rolling his eyeballs toward her. The boobytrap was on the couch between them.

"Do you think we could both get up at the same time?" Rosalie asked.

"Let's not even try it," Framijian said. He cleared his throat and called out, "Help!"

The chimes sounded again, impatiently.

Rosalie called out in a piercing voice, "Whoever it is, please, help us!"

"They can't hear us!" Framijian said. "Save your breath."

"It makes me feel better to scream," Rosalie said.

They heard a scratching sound at the front door.

"What's that?" Rosalie asked.

"They're trying to pick the lock. Not a chance."

After a while they heard a thudding noise, as of something heavy crashing into the door. There was the sound of a motor. Then the sound again, this time much louder. Framijian and Rosalie cringed back carefully. The door came off its hinges and fell across the living-room rug. It was replaced by a rectangle of brilliant sunshine, partially blocked by the white and chrome of a late-model Buick Bushmaster, considerably dented since it had been used to ram the door.

"I think I'm going to faint!" Rosalie said.

"Not yet," Framijian told her. "We got a booby trap here, remember?"

"That's why I'm going to faint!"

"Hold out a little longer!"

The car backed out. Two men rushed in the door. One of them wore a white guayabera shirt, the other a purple-and-gold short-sleeved sports shirt. They had guns in their hands.

"Stop!" Framijian screamed. "Booby trap!"

The men were in full stride and seemed ready to crash into the couch. At the last moment they reined in.

Alvarez said, "Where's the booby trap?"

"Here on the couch," Framijian said.

"What am I supposed to do with it?"

"Don't do anything with it! One of you hold it in place there so it doesn't move. Alvarez, you help Rosalie and me get up."

Alvarez's helper, Manitas, held on to the booby trap while Alvarez helped Framijian and Rosalie to their feet. He got them outside, well away from the house, then called for Gucciardi to come.

"What do I do with this thing?" Gucciardi called from inside.

"Just put it down—*dolce,* eh?—and come out."

"I'm coming, boss. This doesn't look like any booby trap I ever heard of. I'll just put it down here and—oops!"

The resulting explosion took out the front wall.

After a few minutes of awed silence, Framijian said, "Well, that answers the question was it a real booby trap or not. Come on, Alvarez, let's get moving."

Alvarez was still awed by the explosion and by the

sudden absence of Gucciardi, a young man who had shown a fine aptitude for crime, but had a fatal tendency to clumsiness.

"We got to get those cuffs off you," he said to Framijian.

"Don't worry about them now," Framijian said. "You got a car? Come on, let's move it."

"Where to?"

"I want to find those bastards," Framijian said. "No more Mr. Nice Guy. We're going to blow those suckers away."

"Yitzhak!" Rosalie said. "If you leave now, it's all over!"

"Check us into the Fontainebleau," Framijian said. "We'll need a place to stay while somebody fixes the house."

45 •••••

    Blackwell met Minska at his room at the Hotel Nemo. Minska was cool and businesslike. Blackwell was keyed-up, nervous, a little grim.

"You've got the Rolex on. OK. What about the shrapnel Zippo? OK. Here, take this, too."

He opened a handsomely tooled Florentine leather briefcase which was to be used in case Guzmán paid the rest in cash. He showed Blackwell where to press the handle. Blackwell did so, and a section of the upper case slid open, revealing within, in a form-molded space, a small, very flat Spectre SMG, new from Sites S.p.A. of Italy, capable of firing nine hundred rounds a minute. The small weapon had a pistol stock. Its four-column magazine held fifty rounds.

"Not exactly a sniper's weapon," Minska said. "But useful in a crowd. I don't think they'll find this even if they've got an X-ray machine. It's all plastic except for the barrel. Takes the 9×19 Parabellum load. Sinusoidal rifling protects the barrel from wear. Not that we're too concerned about that at the moment. Cock it like this and the first round is chambered and the hammer stays at full cock. You have to push the decocking lever here to bring the hammer down without firing. Firing is easy. No safety—just a double-action trigger pull. You don't even have to oil this baby. It's built with self-lubricating metals."

Blackwell hefted it. The weapon balanced nicely. He slipped it back into the case, clicked it into place, replaced the lining.

"OK," Blackwell said. He seemed strange to Minska, tense and nervous one moment, apathetic the next.

"Is anything wrong?" Minska wanted to know.

"Not exactly. It's just that—well, it's difficult to just pull out a gun and shoot a man, no matter how badly you know he needs killing."

"I know," Minska said. "It's the cowboy ethic. Let the other guy have a chance. Even let him begin to draw first. Then cut him down with dazzling speed. Cultural conditioning. Don't let it affect you."

"I won't," Blackwell said.

"Remember, you were going to become a mercenary. Mercenaries don't give the other guy a break, either. A mercenary makes a contract to kill, and then he does it. That's exactly what the Hunt does."

"I'll be OK," Blackwell said. "You'll be out there?"

"I'll be right near. You get into any trouble, I'll be backing you. Any hassle at all, I'm covering. Anything you get into, I'll get you out of, so don't worry."

"Minska, I think I'm going to be sick."

"Well, hurry up and get it over with."

Blackwell went to the bathroom. He returned a few minutes later.

"You upchuck?" Minska asked.

"Just some dry heaves. I'm OK now. But I think this is my last Hunt as well as my first."

"The first is always the toughest," Minska said. "It's time. Get going."

"Here's looking at you, kid," Blackwell said, for no evident reason, and went out the door and got in his rented car and drove off.

Minska watched him go. All the best ones had temperament. They were as bad as actors, these Hunters. He just hoped Blackwell could get the job done. And that everything would turn out all right. He liked Blackwell. He felt bad that there were a few things he hadn't been able to tell him. The Hunt Corporation played some wily games.

46 • • • • •

"If that fag tries that again," Coelli said, "I'm going to flatten him."

"He's no fag," Blake said. "Lots of Latin guys wear those ruffled shirts."

"Do they also squeeze your ass?"

"He was just trying to make you feel at home. Stay cool."

Blake and Coelli had arrived at the party in Blake's year-old Toyota. It looked like a pile of shit alongside the Maseratis and Ferraris, to say nothing of the Cadillacs and Buicks. There were a couple of guys doing nothing but parking the cars. A lot of guests were arriving. A lot of the men were wearing ruffled shirts, and the women looked like orchids on high heels.

Tito checked the guests, and when he saw Blake he smiled. "You're not on the guest list, but I guess it's OK."

"It better be," Coelli said. They looked hard at each other, two big men, each with a reputation for meanness to maintain. They exchanged "I'll see you later, baby" looks. Blake waved off the attendant and parked his own iron.

"They do themselves pretty good," Coelli remarked. They were just inside the entrance to the living room. At the far end of the room there was a Brazilian dance band—drums, trumpets, guitars, saxophones, three sizes of drums, the musicians dressed up like Monarch butterflies in molting season, and a lead singer with long black hair and tits that looked like nose cones and one of those harsh, moving voices that set Coelli's teeth on edge and gave him a hard-on.

"Ah," Blake said, "here's our host."

Guzmán came over and shook their hands. "So delighted to see you here, Mr. Blake."

"Pleasure," Blake said. "Everything going along alright?"

"Oh, yes, of course. I don't know if you know everybody."

"Who's the good-looking dame in black velvet?" Coelli asked.

"That's Mercedes Brannigan. She works for the Bahamas Corporation."

"Does she now?" Blake mused.

"And that fellow with the slight stoop and the worried expression on his face is Frank Blackwell, an associate of a mutual acquaintance, Mr. Framijian."

Blake's face took on a thoughtful expression. "Could I speak to you for a moment in private. Al? Wait for me here." He told Coelli.

Coelli watched Blake and Guzmán across the room, then helped himself to a tall, frosted, rum drink. Juanito came up to him. "Good evening," he said.

Coelli nodded, "Which one is Blackwell?"

"That's him across the room," Juanito said.

Coelli looked him over. He didn't look like much. Shouldn't be too much trouble taking him down.

The party had a lot of pace to it, Blackwell had to say that for it. As soon as he was in the door, he found two joints pushed into his hand. Then next thing he knew there was a girl in his face. A grinning, lovely young girl with pretty little bosoms rising from a deep-cut red taffeta dress. "You're just in time," she said.

"Time for what?"

"This," she said, and popped a capsule into his mouth. Blackwell tried to fish it out with a finger, but it broke. Something bitter with a strange aftertaste flooded his tastebuds.

"What was it?" he asked. But she had already gone away to pop a capsule in someone else's mouth.

Coelli wasn't the only one being groped. Mercedes had been to a lot of parties in her time, but never one quite like this one. She moved through the rooms, keeping Blackwell's head in sight. Drunken hands touched her as she went by. She was feeling sweaty and irritable. She'd had a few little hits of cocaine earlier and they had lifted her for a while, but now the rush had passed and she was coming down into the jitters.

A large man with a head of curly black hair seized her firmly by the left breast and said something unintelligible in an obscure patois, Guarani perhaps, to judge from the slight lisping of the fricative *th*. She turned to the man and groped his groin. He grinned in amazed pleasure, then his eyes widened as amazing pain flooded him, overloading his sensory equipment, which was already hyped up on a dubious mixture of cocaine, amphetamine, and methaqualone. His eyes rolled up into his head and he collapsed.

There were plenty of drugs. What's the use of being rich and criminal unless you have a lot of drugs for your guests? The marijuana alone was extraordinary. There were many different varieties available, including two types of Oregon buds, one of which had been cured in an enhancing chemical to further its effect. There were black plastic garbage bags filled with the legendary varieties: Panama Red, Acapulco Gold, Michoacan Green, New Jersey Taupe. Acid was available in sunshine or windowpane. Guzmán was a traditionalist about some things, even a nostalgicist.

Whatever it was the girl in the red taffeta dress had given him, Blackwell was feeling suddenly very good. He was able to attend to the various threads of different conversations that floated on all sides of him, and to find them deeply significant.

". . . told Manolo that the bull hooked to the left, but no, he wouldn't listen; watch this, he says, and with everybody in the Plaza Mexico screaming their heads off, he goes and—"

". . . cranked her right up to a hundred and five miles an hour, so she's bouncing over the wavetops like a goddam flying saucer, and they were dropping out of sight behind me, the fuzz in their little cop boats, top speed of maybe forty-five mph, and I'm coming through the narrow cut past marker five on the Intracoastal Waterway in Surfside when I see ahead of me they've got a line of barrels completely blocking the way. So I—"

". . . so he goes to me, 'Hey, baby, what'll you take to do it Cuban-style?' and I go, 'What's that supposed to mean, Cuban-style?' and he goes, 'Come on in here, baby,' and he takes me into this room with a vat of black beans and a guy stirring them with a machete, and I start to get a bad feeling about the whole scene, you know what I mean, so when he—"

". . . bull comes down like a ton of black meat with

hooves like stamping machines and horns like bolo knives, and there's Manolo, lying flat on his back, the muleta balanced on the soles of his feet, smiling, and the crowd goes absolutely crazy when the bull—"

". . . threw the boat into a broadside turn and dropped a ton of water on them, and then I'm around the other side of the bascule bridge, and I see they got more boats in front of me, and they're opening up with machine guns from the shore only they can't lead me enough because I've cranked the boat till it's going like a Titan booster—"

". . . the beans were only lukewarm, thank God, and then he's climbing into the vat with me right up to his hairy ass in beans, and his friends are standing around pelting us with gardenias and I think to myself, this is not an easy way to earn five hundred bucks, but you can't beat the hours—"

". . . bull still gathering speed charging like greased death on railroad tracks, and the noise from the stand is like Judgment Day cubed and people are falling down in the stands from heart attacks, and Manolo is standing on his head now, waggling the muleta in his teeth, and—"

". . . you want to play rough, I said to myself, you get it rough, and I aimed my boat for the center of their goddam Coast Guard launch and I bailed out. Lucky I had on an Air Force pressure suit, because when you hit the water at speeds in excess of a hundred miles an hour you skip like a goddam flat rock; no feeling in the world like it, definitely a peak experience, though not the sort of thing you want to do all the time—"

". . . does a backflip onto his feet, and then, perfect timing, jumps straight up in the air and the bull passes under him, and he stabs down with the sword as it goes by, and son of a bitch if he doesn't nail that sucker on the spot behind the shoulder about the size of a quarter in diameter, and the sword slides in like a red-hot needle going through butter and the stands explode, and it's just at that moment that General Obregón decides to begin his revolution—"

". . . come back again, he says to me, stuffing a couple of extra hundreds into my blouse, and we'll try it next time Mongolian-style, in a hot pot—"

"Mr. Blackwell, are you having a good time?"

"Fine, fine," Blackwell said, shouting to make himself heard over the five-piece mariachi band that was playing while the Brazilian combo took a break.

"Enjoy," Guzmán said, patting him on the shoulder and disappearing into the crowd.

Blackwell realized that he would never find a better time to put his Victim away. He followed him past the kitchen, where the valets hurried back and forth with trays of kasha varnishkas, roast suckling pig, and steaming yucca, while other valets set out the bottles of fiery *cachaza* that had been brought in by Guzmán's own bootlegger from Bahia, and stirred the vats of black beans and the caldrons of rice, and took the cocktail franks out of the microwave, and popped in the corn puffs, and did all of the other things that valets do.

Blackwell was feeling a little fuzzy. What bothered him was that he couldn't remember why he had taken those drugs earlier. It had been drummed into him at the Hunter training sessions that a man needed to be in full command of his senses when he was out on a kill. There was a natural tendency in human beings to want to overdo things, to want to feel more, get higher, experience the godlike, cold, white burst of the cocaine, the mind-expanding rush of the acid, the dreamland voyage of the great marijuana vintages.

But Blackwell had to deny himself that. Or he was supposed to deny himself that. Or most of it. As far as he could recall, he had taken only the smallest hits, since it would have looked strange if he had turned everything down. Let's see, the capsule, yes, and then that joint the size of a Montecristo Imperator cigar, and a handful from one of the cut-glass bowls filled with choicest cocaine. And also, come to think of it, he had sampled the hashish templeballs, the black ones from Afghanistan as well as the golden ones from Kashmir. It was a lot, but he could handle it; he was OK.

He began to move around the room, floating, really, because he had the feeling that he was at least a foot off the ground, propelling himself along by mind power alone. He could hear two different orchestras playing now—the combo and something strange and Asiatic from the hi-fi.

The setting was perfect: a big crowd, people coming and going, the bodyguards trying to cover too much territory, everybody high or drunk, plenty of loud music to mask the sound of the small gun Blackwell wore on his wrist, the two-shot Rolex which also kept time and was waterproof to a depth of two hundred feet.

Blackwell followed Guzmán, moving easily on feet that seemed to float above the white tile floor. He was getting other funny sensations, too. His head seemed to have gotten very light, and he had the feeling that his neck was stretching. He could see above the crowd, above the maddened throngs of merrymakers. Then he shrank to normal height again and found that he had lost sight of Guzmán. But he had to be up there ahead of him somewhere. There seemed to be an endless number of rooms in this house. It was like those endless corridors in *Last Year at Marienbad*. At last he passed the indoor swimming pool and came to a door to a cabana. He could hear a man's voice inside. Blackwell slipped the safety off his Rolex and went in.

47 • • • • •

"Why, Mr. Blackwell, what are you doing here?" Señora Guzmán asked.

Blackwell, caught unawares, heard himself say, "To catch another glimpse of you, señora."

She stared at him, then burst out into laughter. "You should have been born a Latin—you have the correct impulse: when caught in a mistake, give an amorous excuse. This is Father Philus, who was reading aloud to me from *Souls and Flowers*, a recent book on the life of Father Pedro Murrieta of Chihuahua. Please excuse us, Father. I will converse for a little while with my guest."

Father Philus, a tall, bearded priest, said, "But we just reached the part where Father Murrieta is forced to engage in a staring contest for the life of twenty-five captive nuns with Wahua, chief of the Chiricahua Apaches, known as No-Blinkum."

"I know, but we'll get back to it later."

Father Philus left, somewhat grumpily.

"Tell me what you propose to do with Alfonso," Caterina said.

From the expression on her face Blackwell knew that this woman knew that he was here to kill Guzmán. Many lies flashed through his mind, but he knew they were all futile. It would be impossible to deceive this stern, hawk-nosed, eagle-eyed lady in black.

He tried to think of a temporizing statement. But some strange impulse in his mind made him come right out and say, "Frankly, lady, I was planning to blow him away tonight."

"Oh, good," Doña Caterina said.

"I beg your pardon?"

"Divorce is not permitted us, but sometimes violence is. And there's nothing I can do about your killing him, because you are determined, and if I attempted to stand in your way you'd just kill me and then kill Alfonso anyhow. That is my understanding of how a trained killer works."

"Actually, I was only kidding," Blackwell said.

"I know all about you," Caterina said.

"Well, what are you going to do about it, Señora Guzmán?"

"Do about it? Nothing! I'm overjoyed. I only married Guzmán because of Hector."

"Hector?"

"Hector was my father's son by his first marriage to the notorious Imelda. Hector and I grew up together, and he was always sickly and intellectual and crazy, but we all loved him. But then our father sent him to Paris to the university."

"He did?" Blackwell said.

"Yes, and when Hector got home he had a headful of crazy ideas about people being equal, even Miskito Indians. He threw over the job father had found for him as inspector of cargoes at the port of La Unión and went to Waspam, a miserable place on the Río Coco, where he joined MISURASATA."

"Beg pardon?" Blackwell said. He was beginning to feel unwell. He really should get on with the assassination, but he didn't know how to get away from Doña Caterina without either insulting her or killing her.

"The initials stand for Miskitos, Sumus, Ramas, Sandinistas Working Together. It was a left-wing organization at that time, though later it was taken over by the contras. Well, Hector made some silly speeches on their behalf and was arrested by the Guardia Nacional and sent to the model prison in Managua. No place for a delicate intellectual, Mr. Blackwell. Even healthy peasant-type prisoners rarely survive six months there.

"My father knew that the prison commandant was Colonel Guzmán, and Alfonso's infatuation for me was well known. It dated back to the time we were schoolchildren together in La Escuela de los Mártires on Calle 42 in the suburb of Santiago de Ochoabamba. I took no notice of him, because I was from one of the great families and he was nothing, the son of an Armenian merchant. But we had to save Hector, and so I married Alfonso."

"Say, look," Blackwell said, "it's been great talking to you, but now I really—"

"At first it wasn't so bad," Doña Caterina continued. "Alfonso got Hector to Miami with the help of some of his CIA friends and gave him a nice home near Brandenton with a golf course on one side and a contra training camp on the other. But Hector ran away, and it was six months before we heard from him again, and then we found out he'd been caught trying to rob a Taco Bell in Key Largo in order to raise money for Greenpeace. And now he's in prison in Tallahassee and it's Alfonso's fault for bringing him to Florida in the first place. So if you really want to kill him—Alfonso, I mean—it's all right with me. If you can, that is."

"What do you mean, if I can?"

"Guzmán is a hard man to kill. And unlike you,

Mr. Blackwell, he finds it very easy to kill others.
You may think you are Hunting him, but don't be
too sure. Alfonso has played this game a lot longer
than you."

Blackwell left her and pressed on. Faces swam in
and out of focus, pulsing with the staccato Latin beats
of yet a third orchestra, a group from Haiti, all
drums and flutes and washtubs and hard black tor-
sos in bolero shirts. The room pulsed to rhythms old
when the Panama Canal was still a bog, ancient when
the Suez Canal was born in the determined brain of
the talented de Lesseps, primeval when the Volga
Canal was dug at the cost of millions of peasant
laborers, most of them with beards.

Then, with dreamlike abruptness, Blackwell found
himself in a bedroom. There were low beds covered
with polar-bear spreads. Two or more guests were
buried among the evening wraps, giggling and taking
off clothing, affording a glimpse of silken leg and
tilted breast. Blackwell floated past them, propelling
himself on mind power alone.

He found himself drifting through another passageway, and through a partially opened door, and
inside he could see Guzmán lying on a bed.

Mercedes couldn't find him anywhere. Blackwell
seemed to have vanished, and she went in the direction she thought he had gone. There was a corridor
lit by what appeared to be human arms stuck through
the walls holding flaming torches, showing that
Guzmán's decorator, at least, was a Cocteau fan.

Then she saw him. Blackwell was bent over as
though examining something, something lying on a
bed with polar bears. She drew the small blowgun

from her purse. It looked exactly like a long silver cigarette holder, but the cigarettes it held could not be lit. Their ends were packed with tobacco which concealed the little steel darts backed up by a wadding of lamb's wool. You put the deadly little thing to your lips, aimed it by using your nose as a pointer, and puffed, and the little dart flew out, with its protective coating of tobacco shredding away before the steel tip reached its target. It was a close-rang weapon, just the thing for a party. The back of Blackwell's neck, somewhat in need of a haircut, presented a convenient target. She took a deep breath and put the holder to her lips.

The man was lying facedown on the bed, his small feet in patent-leather dance pumps dangling over the side. It was Guzmán, beyond a doubt, passed out cold, but Blackwell had to make sure. He knew that he must avoid at all costs killing the wrong man, and sometimes, in the excitement of the moment at the time of the Kill, the back of one neck looked remarkably like the back of another neck. Nevertheless he had a weapon ready, not his Rolex but a Smith & Wesson belt buckle with two-shot capacity, one a quick-acting nerve gas, the other a .22 caliber bullet with a soft lead nose dumdummed so that its impact would approximate the damage of a .45 caliber slug at twenty feet. Blackwell clicked the tiny fire selector to gas; no trace would be found.

But first he had to turn the man over to make sure of his identity. "Excuse me, Mr. Guzmán, I wanted to ask you . . ."

He turned the man over. Only it wasn't a man. It was a life-size dummy, a painted replica of Guzmán.

Blackwell stepped back, dumbfounded, and saw Mercedes, a long silly-looking cigarette holder extending from her lips.

"I was just going to thank our host for a lovely evening," Blackwell said, and fell straight down in the rubbery, boneless journey in the elevator of time to the bottom of the world that is a well-known effect of methaqualone, especially in collaboration with other drugs.

48 • • • • •

"Come on," Blake said. "We're getting out of here."

"What's the rush?" Coelli asked, his mouth full of kasha varnishka. "This Cuban food or whatever it is is pretty good."

"Take a few with you in a napkin."

Outside, in their car, Coelli lit up a cigarette and settled back in his seat. "I thought we were supposed to do something about that Blackwell guy."

"That's being taken care of," Blake said.

"Then why are we sitting out here?"

"It's agency policy not to be around when the messy stuff begins."

"Then why not leave?"

"I like to watch."

49 ● ● ● ● ●

Blackwell was having a nice dream. There was something blue in his dream, and something about a big dog, and there was a girl in it, too, a girl like Mercedes, but it wasn't exactly her. It was a comfortable dream, and it had felt like it was going on for a long time. Some dreams are so satisfying, you just don't want to interrupt them and get on with real life. You even question how real this so-called real life is. You remember Chuang-tze dreaming he was a butterfly, then waking up and wondering if he was Chuang-tze or the butterfly. And here was Blackwell waking up and for a moment lying there with his eyes closed and considering the possibility of just never opening them. Because he had a feeling, a presentiment, that when he opened his eyes he was going to find himself in a lot of trouble.

He sat up. He was lying on a cot made up with a brightly colored Mexican blanket. He was in a small room, one he had never seen before. There was a two-year-old calendar on the wall from some *carnicería* in Hialeah. It had a photograph of the Plaza Mayor in Madrid on its upper half. The room had one window, but it had heavy wooden shutters over it locked with a padlock. There was a makeup table with a Spanish-language movie magazine on it. *Novedades*. He got up, went to the door. It was locked. He looked around. There was a closet. He opened it. It was filled with a lot of frilly-looking girl's clothing.

He sat down at the vanity table and looked at himself in the mirror. A little the worse for wear. He had an ache in his right knee. Must have fallen on it when he passed out.

The next question was, where was he? Someone else was going to have to answer that one, because he didn't have a clue. Well, he had one or two clues, maybe. To judge by the evidence, he was being held prisoner by a young Spanish-speaking girl who liked to wear a lot of thin cotton blouses. So much for the evidence.

He walked up and down the room, then sat down on the bed. Someone else was going to have to make the next move.

50 • • • • •

Guzmán was sitting at his desk watching Blackwell on a small TV monitor. He had installed the little concealed TV camera in the room back in the days when Conchita, prettiest maid he'd had around for a long time, was working for him and sleeping in there. Guzmán said he installed the hidden camera because he suspected Conchita of stealing silverware. But everyone in the household knew he just liked to watch her undress. Conchita left after a while, and the other maid, Francesca, was sleeping in the other maid's room on the far side of the house over the garage. So this room had been vacant and came in real handy for prisoners. Guzmán was pleased that he had found a use for it other than checking out Conchita's cone-shaped breasts with the large purple-brown aureoles. Now he could use it for checking out Blackwell.

Guzmán rolled a huge joint for himself, using five Bambú papers. He sprinkled cocaine over it liberally, then glued it together with hashish oil. Guzmán didn't indulge often, but when he did, he liked to feel some effect. "Is he awake yet?"

Tito turned from the TV screen. "Just coming around now."

"Now then, I want everyone to understand. No mention of the Hunters. It is apparent that Blackwell doesn't think I know about his connection with them. We are going to act as if he's still a dealer in our good graces. We will pretend to believe that Framijian tried to pull a fast one. As a matter of fact, it's possible that that's exactly what Framijian did. We've checked out our sources. Various weapons did leave the government warehouse in Opa-Laka. The question is, where are they now? Another question is, where is my nine million dollars advance money? So let Blackwell believe everything is OK. Let him think he still has a chance to walk out of here alive. We won't let him out of our sight until we have the guns or the money. Preferably both. Then we cancel him."

"But what if he won't talk?"

"I think we can get him to talk. Mercedes, what do you think?"

Mercedes had been sitting across the room, sipping soda water and frowning.

"From the point of view of the Bahamas Corporation," Mercedes said, "what is important is to know who employs him, who set this up. It would also be interesting to know whether this operation was aimed primarily at you or at us."

"Can there be any doubt?" Guzmán asked. "The man is obviously Hunting me!"

"I don't think it's obvious at all," Mercedes said. "He's had several chances to kill you. He's exposed himself more than necessary if he's merely or exclusively hunting you."

"Then who's the Hunter?" Guzmán asked.

"What makes you think there *is* a Hunter? You get one crank letter and you act like the cossacks are at the door."

"Cossacks? What cossacks?" Doña Caterina asked.

"Please don't use figures of speech around my wife," Guzmán said. "She doesn't understand them.

Look, I wouldn't want the Bahamas Corporation to think I'm not cooperating. What we're going to do, we're going to have a late dinner with Mr. Blackwell and ask him a few questions in a nice way."

"And suppose he doesn't answer?"

"Then we try some ways that are not so nice."

51 •••••

And so the family gathered for dinner. Nothing special, just a little snack here in the kitchen; we'll serve ourselves since we've sent the butler and his children away for a couple of days to Disneyland. Just family here: Alfonso, Caterina, Juanito, Tito, Emilio, and Chaco, and of course our esteemed guests, Mercedes and Frank.

Juanito serves the food, leftover Chinese; we just warm it up in the microwave—we've got plenty. Spare ribs Chinese-style, cooked in something that tastes like orange marmalade mixed with soy sauce. Other things which consist of cardboard cartons filled with celery sliced diagonally swimming in sauce. And Key lime fortune cookies for dessert.

Mercedes present, munching thoughtfully, her face a study in expressionlessness.

All very civilized in the tile kitchen with the Danish porcelain stove, the microwave, the Cuisinart, the dishwasher, and all the rest of the gadgets.

Blackwell eats lightly, figuring people are going to be dancing on his stomach soon. Nice to get a breather, but he doesn't like to think about what lies ahead.

"We want no difficulties," Guzmán says.

Guzmán is the epitome of friendliness, concern. "I don't know what you've heard about me, but it is all lies. I did what I had to do, no more, no less. Now

I stand for frank talk and square dealing. We need not be enemies. All you have to do is tell us where the weapons are. Also, where you put that check for nine million. We can work it all out. We can do business together. I could use a smart young fellow like you in my organization. There's a lot of money to be made here. What do you say, Frank?"

It was a pleasant sort of a moment. It really was like being with family, sitting around with Guzmán and Caterina, with Mercedes across the table from him. It occurred to Blackwell that he could do all right for himself in Guzmán's organization. He could forget Claire, forget the Hunters, forget Minska, could save his life and get on with the next thing, whatever that was. And he was tempted. He knew what was going to come after this. He was going to hurt. And after that he was going to be dead.

They were waiting for his answer. He looked at their faces. Such nice people. This was the crisis, the moment that comes to Hunters. Simmons had told him about it. There comes a time, after long association with your Victim, when you begin to see things his way. Identify with him. Sympathize with him.

Guzmán was being reasonable. What could be so bad about that?

Feeling this way, Blackwell was surprised to hear himself say, "Eat shit and die, Guzmán."

Then Tito swiped him over the head with an automatic and it was blackoutsville again.

52 •••••

While the men carried Blackwell to a different room in the basement, Mercedes and Caterina looked at each other across the kitchen table.

"So what are you going to do?" Doña Caterina asked. "What is your business with that man?"

Sometimes, late at night, in times of stress, far from home, two women can talk with a candor that would astonish them both in other times.

"I'm supposed to find out who he is and who he works for."

"And then?"

Mercedes sighed and shrugged. "*Finito.*"

"I thought as much."

"Trouble is, I've gotten sorta fond of the guy."

"Then how can you kill him?"

"Well, it's my job, you know. I mean, it's nothing personal."

"But what about love?"

"Well, what about it?"

"Isn't love worth something?"

"What on earth are you talking about?"

"The emotion that you feel for this man. It is called love, my child."

"That's ridiculous," Mercedes said. "A one-night stand, that's all."

"The way you looked at him when he fell to the

225

floor after Tito hit him argued more emotion than you admit to."

Mercedes pursed her lips. "He *is* sort of cute. If I had my way, maybe I'd let him live. But I'd have everyone down on my neck if I did that. And I'd be giving up my future. My present, too, come to that, if you know anything about the Bahamas Corporation."

Caterina shrugged. She got up and started to walk away, then stopped and said, "He loves you, you know."

"How could you possibly know a thing like that?"

"Earlier, when he was recovering consciousness, he kept on saying your name."

"He did? Really?"

"Yes. Over and over."

"What did he say?"

"He said, 'Claire, Claire . . .' "

"Oh, for God's sake," Mercedes said.

"Or perhaps it was 'Clear, clear.' Sometimes I do not understand so good the English."

"It doesn't matter," Mercedes said, and hoped she believed that.

53 •••••

In the Hunt headquarters beneath northern New Jersey, a telephone rang. The duty man on the switchboard took it. His lips pursed as the caller identified himself. Swiftly he transferred the call to the private chamber of the Huntmaster.

Minutes later, the telephone rang in the lavishly furnished bedroom that Simmons occupied.

"Yes, Huntmaster . . . . Yes, I understand."

Well-disciplined, Simmons asked no questions. He arose and dressed quickly. Then he telephoned to the Hunt's private air facility.

"Grigory? Get the jet ready. The Huntmaster and I will be taking off in half an hour."

That done, he made one last call. This one was to the Hunt's secret European headquarters in an old warehouse in Basel, Switzerland. He identified himself and then spoke the fateful words. "In the morning, at 0700 hours your time, begin Plan Dioscuri."

He waited until the instruction had been repeated and confirmed. Then he hung up.

His face showed no change of expression, but he could feel his heart pounding like a triphammer. This was it, the big one. The Huntmaster was going for all the marbles.

54 • • • • •

"Did you know it's four in the morning?" Coelli asked.

Blake lit another long, thin cigar. "So what?"

"So we been sitting in this driveway outside Guzmán's house for three hours."

"So?"

"So I got to go to the bathroom."

"You can sneak a pee outside in front of the car," Blake said.

"Somebody'll see me get out."

Blake shook his head. "I've got the overhead light disabled. Just keep your head down."

"I don't see why we're sitting here," Coelli said. "I thought you said Guzmán was taking care of the problem."

"Maybe Guzmán doesn't know exactly what the problem is," Blake replied.

Coelli found that intriguing, but Blake didn't expand on it.

While Coelli was peeing against the fender of Blake's Toyota, he saw a shooting star and made a wish. He wished he had gone to Baltimore to play Class AA baseball instead of accepting the agency offer. But now it was too late.

55 • • • • •

"Hey, boss, look at this one," Tito said, holding out the gaily colored comic book.

Tito and Guzmán were alone in the den discussing torture. Torture was man's work, and so the women had stayed in the kitchen to chat about whatever it is women talk about when their men are planning tortures.

Even Juanito had been sent away. He was too young.

"What is it?" Guzmán asked.

"It's this really neat torture in this issue of *Torture Comics*. But you need some equipment. A pit. And a pendulum."

"Forget it. We don't have time for big production tortures."

"Can't we at least do the Iron Worm and the Green Leaf like we used to do back in Managua?"

Guzmán shook his head. "That's a really great torture, but it needs bamboo slivers. Our oriental food store doesn't carry them."

"What about the Rat and the Sinking Ship?"

"Same trouble. Special equipment. Where are we supposed to find caulking compound at this hour?"

Tito thought hard, and his face showed the strain. Then his expression brightened. "I know! I'll get my Black & Decker and we'll show this guy how we play Nose Dentistry!"

"I can't stand the sound the drill makes as it bores through the septum," Guzmán said. "No, I'll never forget what this Mafia guy told me. He said, all you need is a blowtorch and a pair of pliers and anybody's going to tell you anything."

"Hell, we got those right downstairs in the workroom," Tito said. "I'll go get them."

Guzmán blew a plume of smoke from his cigar. He had just begun the cigar, and it was burning perfectly.

"Well, give him a few more minutes," Guzmán said. "And we might as well see if Dr. Machado-Ropas's new system of psychological torture has any merit." Guzmán turned in his swivel chair to the stacked row of hi-fi equipment. He selected a tape from a file marked "Special-Purpose Tapes," fit it into the machine, turned a switch.

Blackwell returned to consciousness in a room about fifteen feet long by ten wide. The walls and ceiling were covered with sheet metal. The floor was poured concrete and sloped toward the center, in which there was a drain. There were metal cabinets on the wall, securely bolted. There was a single big light overhead, screened behind Plexiglas. To one side, there was a neatly coiled red plastic hose attached to a water faucet.

There was a loudspeaker on one wall, with a button below it. A voice with a faint Spanish accent came over the speaker: "Attention, please. You are in the torture room. Here you will be subjected to unspeakable torments. These will be very bad for you. Medical science concurs in stating that torture is bad for your health, can result in permanent injury or even death. You have been silly enough to put yourself into this situation. Why not be sensible now and make it easy on yourself? The people who have put you here want certain information from you. Do yourself the favor of agreeing to tell, forthrightly and with complete candor, the true answers to anything that is asked. If you agree, please press the button below the loudspeaker and someone will come to take your statement. If you do not press the button, the first torture session begins in approximately fifteen minutes."

Blackwell looked around. There seemed to be nothing he could use as a weapon. Except for the red hose. And his training hadn't taught him how to make a plastic hose into a deadly weapon, if, indeed, such was possible. There wasn't even anything to hide behind so he could spring out and overpower whoever came into the cell. The only thing he could do was rush straight at whoever opened the door and force him to shoot him. That wasn't very satisfactory, but at least it would take care of the torture. Maybe a better idea would occur to him later.

He stood against the wall, bracing his feet, ready for a last run.

Guzmán took a final luxurious puff on his cigar, tamped it out lightly in an ashtray, and stood up. "Time we got on with it," he said to Tito.

"I'm ready, boss," Tito said, smiling and bounding to his feet. "Don't worry, I'll think of something good."

"No doubt. But I don't want you to make a mess."

"You don't?"

"Certainly not. The maids refuse to clean up after messy torturings. Only make a mess if it is strictly necessary in order to get the information out of him."

Pain without mess. Tito found it an interesting

notion. Challenging. But he was up to it. He strode to the door.

Suddenly Blackwell heard the harsh grating sound of a key in the lock. He braced himself against the far wall, ready to rush when the door opened. It opened. Blackwell rushed blindly, and crashed into Señora Guzmán.

Even sprawled on her back with her skirt twisted around to reveal white thighs and black cotton underwear with tiny white crosses appliquéd on them, Doña Caterina never lost her dignity. She straightened out her clothing and got to her feet.

"What are you doing here?" Blackwell asked.

"I have come to rescue you."

"You have? But why?"

"God told me to do it."

"Oh. That's all right, then. What do we do?"

"Follow me, and be very quiet."

Blackwell followed her into the corridor.

They tiptoed down the worn linoleum, under the harsh glare of the overhead lights. Juanito was waiting for them, standing beside the servants' entrance in a white angora sweater with the sleeves pushed back to reveal his slender, muscular, hairless forearms.

Then they heard the sound of pounding footsteps on the stairway behind them. A bellow of rage from inside. A babble of angry voices.

"Come on!" Juanito said. He ran to a car, Blackwell following. A back door swung open. Blackwell dove in, over the man in the backseat, and Juanito slammed the door and ran back toward the house. The driver floored the accelerator and raced toward the gates. Two men with submachine guns materialized in front of them. The driver didn't deviate from his course. He caught one man on the left-side front fender.

Blackwell heard him shriek as he was pitched into the air.

And then they were racing down a dark road, a canal on the right. Blackwell said, "You guys got here just in time. Minska, is that you up front?"

The driver turned, his dark face leering in a dark gloat made all the more sinister by the panama hat perched jauntily on the back of his head.

"No," Alvarez said, "it's just me and another of your buddies."

As they passed a streetlight Blackwell made out the features of the man sitting beside him. It was Framijian. He dug Blackwell in the ribs with something blunt and metallic that had to be presumed to be a handgun of some sort.

56 • • • • •

Dawn was coming up, bloody-fingered on the horizon. Alvarez moved the big car quickly through light traffic on U.S. 1 going south. Framijian was humming "Hatikvah." The interior smelled faintly of contraband Cuban cigars.

"How did you guys happen to be there?" Blackwell asked.

"No disrespect to Don Alfonso, but he's apt to get carried away and end up with a corpse and no information. We've got vital interests in this. We decided to give you a chance to help us."

"Help you? What do you mean?"

"That buddy of yours who camped out in my house has hijacked about ten million dollars' worth of my merchandise," Framijian said. "And I haven't been paid yet because Alfonso gave his check to you."

From the front seat, Alvarez said, "We don't like that sort of thing, and frankly, the people we work for like it even less."

"We want you to help us put everything right," Framijian said. "And quickly, too. You can start out by telling us who in hell you are and why you're coming after Guzmán."

"I'm just an aggrieved citizen," Blackwell said. "You know how it is."

"You're a Hunter, right?"

"Hunter? What are you talking about?"

"Guzmán checked up when those Hunt people sent him that letter. We know all about it. You're the Hunter, stands to reason. Well, tough shit, buddy, your own people have set you up. You better talk to us."

The two men waited while the car's air conditioner quietly pumped out the unbearable real air of Florida and replaced it with the much more satisfactory refrigerated variety.

They were coming into the Homestead area. The low, flat, desolate landscape of the Everglades stretched on either side of them, broken only by billboards advertising Dell Ford, Holiday Inn, the Parrot Jungle, Dade Auto Parts, McDonald's, Computer Express. The sky was an early-morning denim-blue, the horizon was fringed with clouds. They passed Samurai, Featuring Twilight Steak and Chicken Feast for $7.75, The Tamiami Gun Shop, Wendy's, Famous Wall Coverings Factory Outlet, Video City, and Dixie Ribs Barbecue with Parking in Rear. They turned onto two-lane blacktop, palm trees on either side, a few houses. The sky was beginning to darken; wind flurries shook the car.

Ahead of them, a solitary diner loomed, low and wretched on the flat horizon. It's red neon sign spelled out, "Sallil's Shishkaburgers."

"This is the place," Framijian said.

Alvarez turned in and parked. His was the only car in the parking lot.

"We're going to go in here and have a little talk," Framijian said. "The owner is a friend of ours. He won't mind what we do to you."

"If you cooperate," Alvarez said, "we might even buy you a hamburger."

"But if you don't," Framijian said, "we'll turn you into hamburger."

Under a lowering sky filled with scudding black clouds they marched Blackwell into the diner.

57 • • • • •

Blake and Coelli had been following Alvarez and Framijian at a discreet distance. "Pull over here," Blake said. Coelli pulled up across the road from Sallil's Shishkaburgers, where Alvarez had parked. They watched as, minutes later, a blue BMW pulled in near Alvarez's white Lincoln.

"This is interesting," Blake said. "Call Research Division and get me a make on those license plates."

Coelli punched the call into the car telephone. "Myra? How you doin'? Listen, sweetheart, see if you can get me a make on these license plates." He put 7 30 Zeiss wide-angle binoculars to his eyes and read off the numbers. "And make it snappy, will you? We're sitting here with a Code 16 and we don't know who to take down yet."

"They're getting out of the car," Blake said. "Two guys."

He snapped open the hidden compartment under the dashboard and took out a long-barreled L-25 Parabellum he used for serious shooting at middle distances. For serious shooting over demanding distances he had a Winchester 400 in a roofrack above his head. It had a ten-power Bausch & Lomb nightscope already in place.

Coelli had already taken out his automatic, a prototype M1911A2, the new-model update which had been developed in secret after the grand old Colt .45

237

1911A1 was dumped in favor of the reliable but uninteresting 9mm 9ZSB-F. Coelli's friends at Fort Ord had gotten one of the new Colts for him, but he hadn't been able to get one yet for Blake.

Coelli said, "Yeah, go ahead, Myra. OK, thanks." He hung up. "She's a pretty good woman, Myra," he remarked to Blake. "If only she didn't wear those black sneakers all the time."

"*De gustibus,*" Blake said absently, studying the front of the diner through the Bausch & Lomb glasses.

"You want we should go in there and see what's happening?" Coelli asked.

Blake shook his head. "It's going to be a mess. Let's just sit and watch this one."

"Fine with me," Coelli said. "I know that place. The shishkaburgers are really bad."

58 • • • • •

Sallil Bey was a large Lebanese of middle years whose childhood dreams of business enterprises in exotic Western cities had not encompassed ownership of a lousy hamburger joint on a nondescript stretch of road somewhere between Homestead and the Everglades.

He had not bargained for this when he came to America from the bombed-out ruins of Souk el-Farah near Tyre, to join his cousin Immi, the big wheeler and dealer from Tripoli, to find riches in Miami, the Lebanon of America. Only to find himself trapped in a sleaze palace set in a cracked concrete parking lot halfway between nowhere and nowhere south. Not only was he stuck here, but he also had to take care of Jamshid, his uncle's idiot nephew, whom he had promised to watch out for in return for airfare to the States. And he also had his wife, Laila, on his hands, fat, placid Laila with the moon face and the slight black mustache, who, put up against the long-legged beauties of the sun coast with their breasts like doves and their haunches like young foals, rated as a distinct subspecies from a world he had turned from in disgust yet still longed for in his heart of hearts. And now he had a girlfriend living in a trailer camp in Key Largo, whom he supported on the money people like Alvarez and Framijian paid him to provide a safe place where they could disappear people. But now Bettina Sue was getting impatient, asking him to come live with her and invest his savings in a dope-smuggling operation run by a friend of hers. What was he to do? He would have to discuss it with Imrak, the guru of the local chapter of the Hadji Wisdom and Action Group.

The three men were sitting in one of his red leatherette booths and arguing. So vehement was their discussion that they didn't hear the BMW pull into the parking lot. Sallil thought about telling them, but decided against it: no one paid him to report on the arrival of BMWs, or of the other cars that were following the BMW.

Then one of the men from the BMW entered. He was carrying something with which Sallil was all too familiar: an AK-47. Sallil dove for the sheltered spot under the serving counter as a row of glassware exploded along the back wall.

Alvarez, reacting fast, took out the gunner, Chaco, as he came through the doorway with blazing AK-47. Bullets from Alvarez's MAG 50 danced across the Formica tables, smashed the jukebox as it was playing Cyndi Lauper's "Girls Just Want to Have Fun," punched Chaco against the tiled wall, and danced him around until he collapsed into his constituent elements of rayon, shoe leather, black beans, and a Sky-Hi malted.

Tito, an automatic shotgun in his hands, jumped into the room over Chaco's body, his brown face twisted into a grin that showed his rearmost silver-filled molars. He cut down Alvarez in a stench of cordite and brown gravy, and was blown down by Framijian, firing from under the table with an Uzi.

Blackwell ran out through the side door of the café

into the parking lot. Men were coming after him, running hard, shouting at him to stop. He raced to the Lincoln and found the keys in the ignition. Bullets screaming around him; he threw the car into drive and took off.

59 • • • • •

The Lincoln went pretty good, but a gunmetal-gray Lamborghini was gaining fast on him. Blackwell fished around the glove compartment and found a nickel-plated Smith & Wesson .38 with a two-inch barrel. He slipped it into his pocket. Gusts of rain whipped the windshield, and there was nothing much around except landscape. The two-lane blacktop widened ahead to permit a passing lane. The Lamborghini came up fast on his left. When its front bumper was only inches from his tailpipe, Blackwell cut hard into its path. The Lamborghini had to brake, fishtailing to a stop. Blackwell made a screaming turn on two wheels and found himself on a dusty secondary road.

But the Lamborghini was still behind him, and as it came alongside, Blackwell cranked the Lincoln hard to the left again, a maneuver that had worked for him once. The Lincoln rocked up on two wheels, slued its rear end, groaned and creaked with unhappiness, but managed to come down on its wheels. The Lamborghini dropped back, spinning out of control, just managing to stay upright.

Blackwell was just congratulating himself on his maneuvers when his Lincoln lost a wheel and skidded off the road and into the Everglades.

PART SIX

THE BIG KILL

60 • • • • •

Dickerson was sitting in his office studying secret reports. He spent a lot of time doing that because he needed to know many secrets and their various grades—top, restricted, for your eyes only, cosmic, and so on. He also had to remember which secrets had been declassified and therefore could be talked about guardedly with one's friends and neighbors. But sometimes it was difficult to remember which matters were still secret and which had been desecretized, especially when you have to use up some of your memory remembering things like your name, social security number, home address and telephone number, shopping list for the day, names of friends, wives, children, the evening's television listings, political and religious convictions, and so forth. Dickerson was always afraid he was overtaxing his memory by demanding that it discriminate between too many secrets and unsecrets, and that one day the damned thing would malfunction and he would forget what he most needed to remember—inadvertently blurt out to his barber, for example, did you know that one of our moles is now minister of finance of Somalia? Pretty good going for a local boy, wouldn't you say?

Dickerson would never actually reveal anything like that, of course, because he never discussed business, never indulged in idle conversation, never got drunk or stoned. And thanks to a special arrangement he had made with his subconscious, he didn't even have slips of the tongue. But the possibility of catastrophic error preoccupied him all the same. The more new secrets he had to remember but not speak about, the more there came over him a perverse desire, almost a compulsion, to blurt them all out, debrief himself to the world at large, tell his deepest secrets to some casual acquaintance in a bar, or even, horror of horrors, the ultimate faux pas, to seek out one of the KGB people he knew, invite him out for lunch, and then say to him, "I'll show you mine if you'll show me yours."

Such a thing would be unthinkable, of course, and he would never do it. But why did he continually fantasize about it? His psychiatrist, Dr. Mensch, called it the lure of the perverse. Just relax, Mensch told him, the harder you resist the urge to confess the more powerful it becomes.

Just relax, that was easy enough for Mensch to say, but he didn't have the problem of real secrets; all he had was people's dirty little quirks and foibles, not matters of national security.

Dickerson talked with Mensch about his problem with secrets, but he never told Mensch any of them, even though Mensch was a loyal and reliable citizen according to the security check Dickerson had had run on him, before he started therapy under the guise of seeking relief from psychosomatic allergies. The man was loyal, no doubt, but he didn't have a security clearance, wasn't even authorized to know that Dickerson had secrets.

Dickerson's job had become even more difficult because of the new bureau chief. The very identity of this man was a secret. Dickerson had never met him, knew him only through telephone conversations, after the exchange of elaborate identification codes that changed every day.

Dickerson was especially nervous now because the chief had called him yesterday, telling him, in his rough, grating, Chicago-accented voice—probably feigned—to be ready to move immediately; something big was coming up.

Dickerson watched the telephone like a man looking at a sleeping cobra. It could spring into virulent life at any moment, bite him with its hollow fangs, flood his system with the intellectual equivalent of poison, force him to leave the tried-and-true path of safe routine and jump into the dangerous and unpredictable unknown.

He had just about convinced himself that nothing was going to happen, the phone wasn't going to ring, the chief had just been testing him. Didn't someone say that watched telephones never rang?

Then the red telephone rang.

Dickerson's heart gave a tremendous lurch. He closed his eyes, composing himself by reciting the mantra Dr. Mensch had given him: "Om mane padme hum, I smell the blood of an Englishmun." Funny how so simple a sentiment could bring a sense of relief, no matter how short-lived.

He picked up the telephone. "Dickerson here." He listened intently as the grating voice recited the day's recognition code. Then he gave his part of the code, and the real conversation could begin.

"Yes, sir. Right, sir. Excuse me, sir, would you mind running that by me again? Yes sir, I got it."

When he put down the phone his hand was shaking. He repeated his mantra, calming himself. Then he picked up the yellow phone and called Blake in his car.

"Blake? You and Coelli get to the airport immediately. You know which one. Just drop everything and get going. I'll see you there in half an hour."

Dickerson hung up and sighed deeply. The time he had long dreaded had come at last. He was going to meet the chief in person. And he was going to learn more than he perhaps cared to know about what was really going on.

He punched the intercom. "Miss Moneypenny, have Friedrich bring my car around to the side entrance. And hold my calls. No, I don't know when I'll be back."

Or even if, for that matter.

61 • • • • •

Zale had landed in some odd places before in the line of company business, but this one was downright dangerous. He brought the company jet down for a bumpy landing on the small landing field of crushed white shell. They were on the extreme southern end of Outer Cay. Dickerson, Blake, and Coelli unstrapped.

"Zale, you stay with the plane," Dickerson told the pilot. "Keep her ready for immediate takeoff. This meeting might not be entirely friendly."

Zale nodded, but he wondered how Dickerson expected to get back to the jet if the people he was meeting here didn't want him to. And if they didn't want the jet to go, one man armed with a bazooka and stationed in the dense jungle growth that bordered the airstrip would be enough to stop it. But, well-trained operative that he was, he kept his thoughts to himself, reserving them for his memoirs.

Blake and Coelli checked the loads in their Spectre submachine guns. "I just hope he knows what he's doing," Coelli said, *sotto voce*, to Blake.

"What was that?" Dickerson said, picking it up with a superacute hearing.

"I said the groundhog needs rescrewing," Coelli said.

"And just what is that supposed to mean?" Dickerson said.

Coelli looked blank. Invention failed him. Blake stepped in. "He's talking about guns, sir. The ground-hog is what they call the retaining ring of the cluster assembly of the new MCX."

"It's no time for idle conversation," Dickerson said. "I'm going to need you men to back me up. Just stay alert and keep your eyes open and don't do anything unless it's absolutely necessary. But if you must shoot, don't stop until we're back on the plane."

Both men cocked the little autofire Spectres and then concealed them under their lightweight jackets.

"Open the door, Zale," Dickerson said.

Zale swung the door open and folded down the ladder.

On the landing strip, standing in front of the ladder, was Dr. Dahl. The director of the local branch of the Bahamas Corporation wore a lightweight batik shirt, which, flapping in the strong sea breeze, revealed no weapon beneath, but did afford a glimpse of a hairy tanned belly.

"Welcome to Outer Cay," Dahl said. "Let me accompany you to the main house, where we have some light refreshment ready."

"Yes, and what else?" Blake whispered to Coelli.

62 • • • • •

Blackwell's car had turned over when it went off the road. It lay on its side ten feet below the roadbed, partly underwater. Blackwell, groggy but not much the worse for wear, climbed out of the two feet of water. He still had the .38 he had found in the glove compartment, and the Rolex watch gun was still on his wrist, though it didn't seem to matter what time it was and there was nothing close enough to shoot at.

He started to scramble up the steep embankment, then stopped when he heard the roar of an engine and the screech of brakes. A car came to a stop on the shoulder above him.

Blackwell looked for a place to hide. He was on the margin of land where Florida Bay meets the Everglades. Looking across the water, he could see several little hammocks, islands just a few inches above the water and crowded with sea grape, tamarind, and mangrove. The bottom was muck, but it was firm enough to permit him to make some progress, though at great exertion. He waded toward the nearest mangrove island, ducking around to its far side as he heard the car doors slam.

A voice came floating across the water. "Hey, Blackwell, you out there?"

Guzmán! Blackwell resisted the desire to call back, "No, I'm not!" He waited, not moving.

Mercedes brought her Porsche to a quick stop behind Guzmán's car. Before leaving the car she opened her bag and checked the load in the long-barreled .357 Magnum. Then she went out to join Guzmán.

Alfonso Guzmán was standing on the edge of the embankment, looking out toward Florida Bay. He was wearing crisp khakis, a Sam Browne belt, a faded olive-drab hunting jacket. He was carrying a .302 Mannlicher with a ten-power scope. In a holster on his chest he carried an Uzi and two extra clips of ammo. He was smiling, a short, pudgy, dark-skinned man who looked like a kid let out of school early. He stroked the shiny butt of the Mannlicher like it was a pet dog and a best friend and a good-looking mistress all rolled into one.

"Hey, Blackwell!" he called. "I know you're in there, hombre. You're the Hunter, aren't you?"

He waited a few moments, the wind tugging at his jacket and tousling his short crisp hair. "Talk to me, Blackwell. If you say you're not the Hunter, I go away, OK? But if you are, maybe it's time you admitted it, huh?"

"Yes!" Blackwell shouted, his voice echoing thinly across the water. "I'm the Hunter! And you're the Victim!"

Guzmán turned to Mercedes. "Stung his pride, you see? Made him give away his location."

He turned back in the direction from which Blackwell's voice had come. "It's all turned around now, hombre! Now I'm the Hunter and you're the Victim. How you like them apples, gringo?"

A dusty BMW pulled up in front of Guzmán's car in a spray of white dust and a splattering of gravel. Emilio climbed out. He was carrying a Winchester with hunting scope. Slung over one shoulder was a sawed-off double-barreled shotgun.

"He's out there, huh?" Emilio said. "Good, let's go get him, *mi coronel.* I'll go right, you go left. He can't be carrying much firepower, the way he's been bouncing around."

"Your plan is good," Guzmán said. "Tactically sound, just as in the old days. But you are going to stay right here, old friend. I'm going in alone."

"Boss, that's maybe not too smart," Emilio said.

"You don't understand," Guzmán said. "This is *mano a mano,* a classic duel to the death. It's also the most fun I've had in ages."

"Now boss," Emilio said. "I know you're a tiger, but don't get carried away. Let me help."

"You can back me up," Guzmán said. "But don't shoot him. He's mine, *tu sabes?* My kill!" He slid down the embankment, shouted, "Blackwell, *yo vengo!*" and started wading toward the mangrove island.

"He was always headstrong," Emilio muttered, admiration evident in his voice. He shook his head, then slid down the embankment and went after Guzmán.

Mercedes, after a moment's hesitation, also slid down the embankment and followed Emilio.

63 ● ● ● ● ●

It was cool inside the meeting room, under the big, slow-turning overhead fans. Dickerson and Dahl took seats at one end of the long table. Blake and Coelli leaned against the rattan-covered wall, ready to go for their weapons if need be. So far, everyone seemed calm. Dahl mixed two tall, beaded rum drinks, tasted one—"Ah, just tart enough"—and handed it to Dickerson.

"Chin-chin," Dickerson said, taking a sip.

"My God, do people still say that?" Dahl asked.

"Never mind what people say. Let's get down to business."

"Certainly. You are Mr. Dickerson, I believe, head of the southern Florida station of Branch Two of the Revised CIA Directive?"

Dickerson nodded curtly. "And you are Dahl, Caribbean area chief for the Bahamas Corporation. We have quite a file on you and your organization."

Dahl smiled. "As we have on you and yours."

"I think I should point out," Dickerson said, "just to get our positions straight, that most of what the Bahamas Corporation does is illegal and subject both to heavy fines and long prison sentences."

"Of course we're illegal," Dahl said. "But in a cause both vital and noble. And nobody can touch us here on our own island. I think, Mr. Dickerson, that you are not in a position to threaten."

"Oh, I wasn't threatening," Dickerson said. "Just trying to make the position clear."

"You call us illegal," Dahl said. "But in fact we were the last, best hope of mankind."

"Well, that is as it may be," Dickerson said. "Now, can we get down to business?"

Dahl looked quizzical. "What are you referring to?"

"Who called this meeting?" Dickerson asked.

"I don't know what you're talking about," Dahl said. "I have received no instruction from my superiors about this. Your arrival was unannounced and unexpected, though you are nonetheless welcome."

The two men stared at each other, Dahl slightly out of breath. An involuntary movement on Dickerson's part—the physical manifestation, perhaps, of his long-suppressed slips of the tongue—turned over his drink. Before the ice cubes hit the table, Blake and Coelli had their weapons out. Overhead, high in the wall, a panel slid open and the long snout of an AK-47 poked out and covered Blake and Coelli.

Then the small service door at the far end of the room opened and through it stepped Zale, Dickerson's pilot, closely followed by two resident scientists from UCLA wearing Snoopy T-shirts.

"What is it, Zale?" Dickerson said testily. "I thought I told you to stay with the ship—sorry, with the plane."

"I thought you should know, sir," Zale said, "that another plane has just landed."

Dickerson and Dahl looked at each other in consternation and wild surmise.

64 • • • • •

A great silence brooded over the bright, hammock-dotted waters where Florida Bay merged into the swampy coastline of the Everglades. Water and land interpenetrated, moist, slimy, and unrepentant under the great wavy-edged white sun. The highway was a dark slash cutting through the gleamy brightness of the shallow water world. Two cars were parked on the shoulder of the road which bisected it. Near and below them, a third car lay on its side in the shallow water. Far out, in the direction of the Gulf of Mexico, a fishing boat, its twin outriggers quivering, sent up a roostertail of white foam as it headed toward Key West. Closer, a small, low-slung bonefishing skiff moved along near the shore, its straw-hatted occupant pushing it along with a pole.

Guzmán had slung the Mannlicher over his shoulder, relying instead on the small autofire Uzi. Holding it at the ready, he waded to the edge of the hammock and peered in. He could see only a little way into the deeply shadowed tangle of ironwood, gumbo limbo, and black mangrove. He stopped. "Hey, Blackwell! Come on out and play!"

"Come in and get me!" Blackwell shouted from the other side of the hammock. "I'm right in here, you obsolete old-world macho son of a bitch!"

"Obsolete? Hell, kid, you aren't even born yet! Ever kill anyone before? Think you can do it?"

He waited. Suddenly Blackwell came wading out from behind his hammock, his face furious, the useless short-barreled .38 in his hand. Guzmán ripped off a blast with the Uzi. Blackwell grunted, his right arm went red, the gun fell from his hand. He reached down to recover it, but Guzmán was firing again and he had to duck behind the mangroves.

65 • • • • •

The door to the big meeting room of the Bahamas Corporation opened. Both Dickerson and Dahl had risen to their feet. They were standing almost side by side. Against the far wall, Blake and Coelli were frozen like a bas-relief from the side of a gangster's sarcophagus.

Through the doorway walked Simmons. Behind him, small and erect and smiling, was the Huntmaster.

"I know who you are," Dahl said slowly. "Our files are exhaustive. But I had not thought we would ever meet."

"You and your people have taken pains to avoid me," the Huntmaster said. "Perhaps that accounts for it."

"We are on different courses," Dahl said. "Our organization is trying to save the world from its short-sighted folly. You and your Hunt are part of the madness."

"Surely you don't really believe that," the Huntmaster said. "We of the Hunt are part of the solution. We offer voluntary murder as a substitute for war. You know that mankind will never be satisfied unless it is killing something. People can't even properly enjoy a landscape unless there's something moving across it that can be shot at. The drives that lead to war and to progress can't be switched off, and we would breed them out of the race only at our peril.

We humans are hunting animals, Dr. Dahl, and we have run out of prey. There is nothing left to kill but each other. And kill we must. Provision must be made so that we can do so in an orderly fashion."

"Rule of law can still be achieved!" Dahl declared.

"You know that it cannot," the Huntmaster said. "Perhaps many centuries from now, but not in the foreseeable future. My dear Dahl, the first, the primary, task is to bring the earth back into ecological balance. That's your task, you and the Bahamas Corporation. Ours is to give people something exciting to do other than war while that is going on. Without us and our Hunt, you and your high-minded scientists will just be another group of dreamers living in an imaginary kingdom of sweet reason while the madness of real politics rages all around you. Be practical, Dahl, let's do something together."

"There *is* something in what you say," Dahl admitted. "I've been aware for some time of the shortcomings inherent in the sane, dispassionate thinking that we scientists advocate. People don't pay any attention. Unless there's an emergency like Love Canal or Chernobyl, the idea of maintaining and upgrading the earth and its ecosystems is not exactly box-office. And yes, people do need something to get passionate about, and better the senseless voluntary killings of the Hunt than the senseless involuntary killings of millions of people in the standardized mode of modern warfare. If it were up to me . . . but it's not. I am only a regional director, just one of ten who make the final decisions for the Bahamas Corporation."

"Might I suggest," the Huntmaster said, "that it's time for a bright fellow like yourself to take over the Supreme Directive of your company? With our help, of course."

Dahl laughed. "It's tempting, Huntmaster, I must admit that. But quite impossible, I assure you."

"Oh, it's within your reach," the Huntmaster said, his little face hunkering down into a smile. "In fact, it's your only workable option. I've taken the liberty of advising your parent organization of your defection to our side."

"They will never believe you!"

"They will. Plan Dioscuri has already gone into operation. Our trained assassin corps are killing your top executives even now."

"You wouldn't dare!" Dahl said.

"Nothing you or I can do will stop it. By evening your company will be headless. Dahl, come on, man, grasp the opportunity. Don't you realize that between us we can take over the government of the United States? We have powerful friends in Congress, as do you. Join us, and be in on the beginning of a new order for mankind."

Dahl's eyes narrowed as he scrutinized his courses of action and found them limited. "Well, after all," he said, "what do I care if a lot of silly fools kill themselves in your Hunt, as long as my colleagues and I can save the world? All right, Huntmaster, I'm with you!"

Dickerson had been listening to this conversation with growing concern. He stepped forward now, a small man made tall by circumstance.

"If you think I'm going to let you get away with this, you're crazy. Blake, Coelli!"

His men drew their weapons. The AK-47 in the wall opening moved around to cover everyone. It looked like all hell was about to break loose.

"Before you do something you will regret," the Huntmaster said, "does Orange Alpha 323 Weepers Snowshoe mean anything to you?"

"It's today's recognition code," Dickerson said. "How in hell did you get it?"

"It was not difficult," the Huntmaster said, his voice changing into the familiar, grating, Chicago-tainted accent that Dickerson knew only too well.

"Boss!" Dickerson said, and his voice was husky.

"You will follow my orders," the Huntmaster said.

"Yes sir. But sir, why exactly are we doing this?"

"It is for the good of the country," the Huntmaster said.

Hearing that, Dickerson relaxed. He had hoped he wasn't engaged in treason, because that would have set up a conflict in him, and Dr. Mensch had advised him to avoid conflicts.

"Now you can see," the Huntmaster said to Dahl, "why our little plan must succeed. All the important forces are lined up on our side. Within a year the Hunt will be legal in America, and the rest of the world will fall to us soon. Then, Dahl, we can devote all our remaining energies to repairing the earth."

Dahl and the Huntmaster shook hands. Simmons, Blake, and Coelli grinned at each other in the manner of men who have just discovered they are on the same side. The hidden man with the AK-47 withdrew it from the window.

Coelli asked, "What about that Hunter?"

"Blackwell?" Simmons asked. "I suppose he has killed his Victim by now."

"It's not as simple as that," Dahl said. "I'm afraid I have some bad news for you. When this began we sent out our enforcer to learn what had happened to our arms dealer and to correct it. I'm afraid that means canceling Mr. Blackwell."

"Is there no way to call the enforcer off?" Simmons asked.

Dahl shook his head. "She is not in radio contact with us."

"In that case," the Huntmaster said, "Blackwell is just going to have to look after himself. I regret this as much as any of you, but some sacrifices must be made if the new order is to succeed."

66 • • • • •

Emilio heard Guzmán's shot and redoubled his efforts to reach the killing ground, yanking each foot out of the suckous mud, losing his shoes but not his determination. Mercedes, following some yards behind, struggled to catch up. The bonefishing skiff drifted closer, and the man in the straw hat stood up to see what was going on.

"Get away!" Emilio shouted, waving his gun.

The bonefisherman turned away, then suddenly swung back. His hat fell off, revealing broad Polack features. Minska! An Uzi in each hand blazed briefly. Emilio crumpled. The bonefishing skiff rocked from the recoil. Minska flailed his arms, trying to keep his balance. At that moment he made a great target. Mercedes took him down with a .357 Magnum slug.

67 •••••

Guzmán waded closer and stopped about three feet away, the Uzi ready in his pudgy hands. Blackwell lay in the shallow water, holding his right arm with his left and trying to stay conscious. The shock was beginning to wear off, and pain was starting to radiate from his smashed shoulder. Behind Guzmán, Mercedes appeared, her white linen suit mud-streaked, her long dark hair in disarray.

"How you like hunting now, *coño?*"

Blackwell didn't reply. What was there to say?

"So long, stupid," Guzmán said, leveling the Uzi.

"No!" Mercedes cried, and fired reflexively. The big slug from her .357 Magnum took out the back of Guzmán's head. He pitched straightforward face first into the water, a human cocktail for the crabs.

Mercedes knelt beside Blackwell. The Magnum was still in her hand, aimed in the general vicinty of Blackwell's head.

"I couldn't let that fat slob shoot you," she said. "That's no way to die, killed by a greaseball who uses Vaseline on his hair."

"Mercedes," Blackwell said, "I love you. This has all been sort of crazy, hasn't it? What say we run away together, just you and me. We'll go somewhere they've never heard about Hunting, like New Guinea. We'll get married and love each other forever and it'll be good. What do you say?"

Her face was tear-streaked. "If only I could!" she said. "I'm crazy about you, Frank. You're so cute and helpless and nice and straightforward. I've never met a man like you. But it would never work, sweetheart. Funny you should mention New Guinea—I've just come from there. I had to rub out a guy who disobeyed the Bahamas Corporation's rules."

"Tell them Guzmán shot me and I disappeared underwater or something, and you looked but you couldn't find me. We'll find some other place even farther away. We'll meet a month from now at the Skidmore Fountain in Portland, Oregon. No one'll think of looking for us there."

"I'd like to do that, darling, but they give us polygraph tests after every mission, to make sure we aren't getting soft. I'm sorry, but better me than some stranger. Close your eyes. You won't feel anything but the impact."

"Mercedes!" Blackwell said. "Stop kidding around!"

She bent over him, lovingly, murderously, and put the gun to his temple. Blackwell got his left hand onto his right wrist and pressed the bezel on his Rolex gun. The shot scorched Mercedes's cheek and clipped off a lock of her dark hair.

"Well," she said, tight-lipped, "maybe you aren't so nice after all."

"Baby, let's talk about it!"

Her lips compressed and her finger tightened on the trigger. Blackwell closed his eyes. A shot rang out.

68 •••••

Six months later, Blackwell came to the secret installation beneath northern New Jersey and descended by elevator to the operations level. The secretaries ushered him through. Simmons came out of his office and accompanied him to the Huntmaster's chamber.

"Delighted to see you, Frank," the Huntmaster said. "Shoulder's healing up all right, is it?"

"It's fine," Blackwell said.

"I suppose you heard on the way here, Congress has just voted into law the Legalized Murder Act combined with the Clean Water, Earth, and Air Act. A new day for mankind has begun at last."

"Yes sir," Blackwell said. "I'm very happy about that."

"Still upset, are you?"

"Yes sir, I am."

"Well, you've held the grudge long enough. I want you two to make up." The Huntmaster gestured. Minska stepped out of the shadows.

"Hiya, kid," he said. "I've been wanting to visit you in the hospital, but they said you didn't want to see me."

Blackwell's face tightened. "I don't want to see you now. You said you'd back me up. But you weren't there when I needed you."

"At least let me tell you why I was late."

266

"I don't want to hear," Blackwell said. "You were my friend and my spotter. I trusted you. And you weren't there."

"It was on my orders," the Huntmaster said. He gestured. Two men stepped out of the gloom behind the shadows. They were small men with white panama hats and small mustaches. They were Valeriano and Panfilo, looking much better than in their contra days on the hillside outside San Francisco de la Paz.

"Forgive your friend, señor," Valeriano said. "He was late because he had to deliver the weapons he had hijacked to us. Yes, he risked your life. But had he not gotten the arms to us in time, it would have meant the failure of the revolution."

"I don't understand," Blackwell said. "I thought the contras lost."

"Of course," Panfilo said. "But *we* never were contras. Valeriano and I have been secret agents of the Hunt since our university days."

"It is true," Valeriano said. "Our underground was able to distribute the entire arms load to our followers. The real uprising began the next day. Men from the Sandinistas and from the contras flocked to our cause. We stood for the great popular ideas of the day, legalized murder, a not too outrageously disproportionate distribution of wealth, and ecological primacy. It is because of your friend, señor, that this very week the Hunt became legal in all the countries of Central America which are united under our rule."

"And after all," Minska said, "I did get there in time to save your life."

"You didn't have to kill her!" Blackwell said.

Minska shook his head. "I had to, Frank. She was going to kill you."

"She was *not* going to kill me. She was just kidding around."

"She was sure as *hell* going to kill you, Frank. And even if she *was* just kidding around, how was I to know that at thirty yards?"

"You could have wounded her instead of killing her."

"Are you kidding? Me lying there with my left leg shot out from under me, drifting in and out of consciousness? You're lucky I hit anywhere near her, state I was in."

Blackwell shook his head. His voice trembled. "Minska, I tell you, she loved me."

Minska put his arm around Blackwell's shoulder. "Maybe she did, kid, maybe she did. But she also had this streak in her, call it a mean streak, because she was sure as hell going to kill you even if she did love you, which, somehow, I doubt."

Blackwell's shoulders drooped. His face fell. The bags of despondency under his eyes were filled with the oily secretions of self-pity. He said, "Well, it's over. First Claire and now Mercedes. What is this bad luck I have with women? They keep on getting killed around me. But what really hurts is that now I don't have anything to look forward to."

"Yes you do, kid." Minska's smile was broad, confidential.

"What are you talking about?"

"Take a look at this." Minska took out a sheet of paper and held it out to him. Blackwell took it, read it, then read it again with growing comprehension.

"A Hunt? We're going out on another Hunt? But I didn't sign up."

"I took the liberty of doing that for you," Minska said. "You can still cancel out, of course. But then I'd have to find someone else to Spot for."

"I don't know that I'm up for another Hunt," Blackwell said. "I didn't do so well on this last one. I mean, it was Mercedes who finally killed the Victim, not me." His voice grew husky. "She killed for me, Minska!"

"Don't start up again, Frank. I know you didn't do so good this last time. But you got the real stuff in you. Trust me, I know about these things. Lot of people it takes them one Hunt just to warm up. This time you're going to dazzle them."

"You really think so?" Blackwell asked, his voice husky.

"You better believe it, kid," Minska said. "Otherwise why would I put my life and reputation on the line by Spotting for you again?"

"All right, Minska," Blackwell said. His voice was under control. "We'll do it again, and this time we'll do it right."

After they had left, and Panfilo and Valeriano had taken the elevator upstairs to the reception in their honor, Simmons said to the Huntmaster, "I'm really glad it has worked out well for Blackwell, sir. One shouldn't get personal about these things, but I was worried about him."

"You needn't have been," the Huntmaster said. "I could have told you from the beginning he had the right stuff. And somehow, the happiness or unhappiness of his individual life, or even its sudden extinction, is nothing compared to the social change he helped to engineer. The Hunt is legal now, Simmons, and all the rules by which mankind has lived are transformed. War is over! The earth is saved! The age of happy endings has come at last!"

About the Author

Robert Sheckley is best known for his off-beat, witty short stories, which he began writing in 1951. He was a protégé of Horace Gold, former editor of *Galaxy*, a magazine in which many of his early stories appeared, and by the mid-1960s, he had already produced a significant body of work that was widely acknowledged to be at the forefront of science fiction. His bestseller, THE TENTH VICTIM, and the subsequent movie, launched his reputation far beyond genre classification. Mr. Sheckley has also had a major influence on his fellow writers as fiction editor of *Omni* magazine. HUNTER/VICTIM is the third book in the series begun with THE TENTH VICTIM and continued with VICTIM PRIME.